BONA

———— *by* ————

KEN WILBUR

authorHOUSE®

AuthorHouse™
1663 Liberty Drive
Bloomington, IN 47403
www.authorhouse.com
Phone: 1 (800) 839-8640

Published by AuthorHouse 02/11/2016

ISBN: 978-1-5049-7891-0 (sc)
ISBN: 978-1-5049-7890-3 (e)

Dedication:

To Sister Blandina Segale; said to have stood up to Billy the Kid. An Italian-born nun who calmed angry mobs and helped to open hospitals and schools in New Mexico. Sister Blandina was the real Maverick Nun and she is moving up the path to possible sainthood.

* * * * * * * * * * * * * * * * * * *

Thank You:

To Rachel Rosenboom for
Proof reading.
To my granddaughter Sarah
For allowing me to use her photos and
For posing for pictures.
To my grandson Andrew for posing
for pictures.
To my daughter Angee for taking photos.
To Alec Cadwell for posing for pictures and
To my son Brent for working with the photos
And taking pictures.

Chapter One

The faint, acrid odor of burning buffalo chips came to the nostrils of Bona King. Following upwind, the scent grew stronger and stronger. He rode slowly over the prairie, a cheroot dead for hours, clamped in his teeth. All was silent but the ceaseless voices of the evening and the dull thudding sounds of Duke's hooves on the hard packed earth.

Bona, came out of the Civil War a changed man. Migrating west he found himself in Texas, on the Rio Grande near the border of New Mexico. He slipped from the back of Duke, his buckskin gelding. As he ground reined Duke, he spoke as if the animal was a human companion.

"Wait here," and then to himself but aloud. "I should know better than to sneak up on a strange camp. Good way to get my damn head blown off." Deft fingers slipped the rawhide off the hammer of his Navy Colt.

Slowly, he worked his way through the twisted and naked trees. They were old, scant of foliage. Clusters of mistletoe grew among the now bare branches. Like a shadow, Bona crept forward to the last bush type tree. Instinctively, his hand checked the Colt on his left hip. He froze, hand poised over the butt of his revolver. He watched the group by the campfire. Patience, he thought. A lesson he had learned well was the futility of haste.

Photo by Sarah

With caution he worked his way toward the ring of light. The forms by the fire motionless. On one side of the fire stood four or five, on the other three faced them. It was unnatural. This was not what he expected or what was reasonable. Moving even more into the open but concealed by the shadows of dusk, Bona worked his way forward. He strained to hear what was being said. He didn't like what he saw in the dim light of the setting sun. He drew his Colt and crept forward, alert for any sign of what was going on.

"No! Not the crucifix! You...."

A flash of fire and the sharp explosive crack of a revolver punctuated the unfinished statement. One of the two black shapeless forms was flung backwards. Arms spread eagle by the force of the slug hitting flesh. His killer thumbed his revolver and shot him again while in mid-air.

Bona still didn't understand the situation but he knew which side he was on. His Colt belched fire and one of the dark forms dropped his gun and grabbed his side as he was twisted around.

At this same time one of the black forms stepped forward only to have a revolver knock it to the ground. Again and again his Colt sent heavy blows of death toward the mass of figures. The distance was too great for accurate shooting but they scatted like a pack of rats. As they dove for cover, a couple shots were fired in the general direction of Bona. A minute later the sound of running horses told him the fight was over for the time being. He moved forward.

"Thank the Lord. We were in dire need of a friend," the voice of a woman spoke with a note of agony. She was kneeling by the limp figures on the ground.

"You still are." Bona pointed and nodded at the forms at her feet. He expressed his question without speaking.

"Father Francis and Sister Esther." Her eyes studied the stranger that saved her from a fate worse than death. He was muscular, with black hair, blue-gray eyes that glinted like steel. He was tall, at least six foot and broad of shoulders. His complexion darkened by long exposure to sun and wind gave him a bronze statue look. His blue denim shirt and trousers were soiled and his face was covered with several days' growth of dark whiskers.

"Well I'll be....." Bona let it die, unfinished. As he recognized the religious habit of flowing black. She was a nun.

"I am Sister Teresa. Father Francis, Sister Esther and I were on our way to Saint Anthony's. That's a mission and orphanage in the Seven Rivers Country." Her pale blue eyes turned bitter as she retold the account of the attack on them.

"We were transporting a gold crucifix to go above the altar. This band of marauders rode into our camp, took the crucifix and shot Father Francis when he attempted to stop them. When Sister Esther stepped forward to help she was clubbed with a gun. Heaven only knows what they would have done to me had you not came to my rescue." Tiny freckles were sprinkled lightly on the bridge of her piquant nose. Her face ringed with a white starched wimple and bib against layers of black was very pretty.

"Thank the Lord for you. Now...." Bona stopped her as he turned his back and whistled, the shrill clear note summoned the buckskin. He stripped the gear from the horse, rubbed him down with a handful of grass and turned him loose to drink and graze.

Only then did he take a tin cup of coffee the nun held for him. He noticed a change in her eyes and the lines around her mouth. It wasn't a pout it was more a defiant look of determination. Her rosary beads dangling from a silver ring and joined at the ends by leather, formed a belt around her tiny waist. With an absent-minded reaction her hand went to the rosary and agile fingers counted the beads.

From a pan on the fire, Bona took a biscuit and some meat to eat with his coffee. The biscuit was dry but he had learned to make due, to eat when he could and rest when he could.

"How can you eat at a time like this?"

"I'm hungry."

"You could show more respect. What do you do?" The question came from where she was kneeling.

"I play poker when I can find a game, I live off the land and travel alone."

"You should grow up, you could make a fine adult." She flung the jeer without looking up.

Bona had to chuckle. She had grit. For all she knew he could be one of the many renegades that roamed the country. The Civil War had put a great deal of bitterness and violence in many a man. It had changed Bona but not to the point of harming a woman or killing a man for no reason. But she did not know that.

He flipped the butt of his cheroot into the fire, put his head on his saddle and pulled a blanket up around his shoulders. Almost at once he was asleep.

Bona woke to the smell of coffee and bacon over the open fire. Sister Teresa was busy making sourdough biscuits. The hot biscuits were delicious, the bacon savory, and the coffee strong and hot. He ate without a word. Wiped the tin plate clean with the last of his biscuit and licked his lips. He used a twig to put fire to a cheroot and leaned back to enjoy his smoke and coffee.

"A heap of dry and wild country between here and Seven Rivers." His slow drawl made it sound as if he were talking to himself.

"The least you could say is thanks. That was the last of the bacon." She spoke from across the fire. All she was having was coffee.

"Thanks." His eyes hard on hers. She had not slept and it showed. A touch of angry color began to creep into her cheeks as she looked away.

"I'll dig some graves while you pack." Bona rose and walked to a likely spot for the graves. Using a stick and a large flat rock he scraped out shallow graves. He lifted the priest, bedroll and all and placed him is his final resting place. He did the same for the Sister. Using his feet he did what he could to cover their bodies. He placed rocks all over the mounds of dirt.

"Is that the best you could do?" A hint of anger laced her question.

"Makes little difference to them now."

Her eyes blazed and there was a moment of hesitation before she answered. "V'algame Dios." She snapped as she knell by the graves.

"God help you? He didn't do much for these two, why should he help the likes of me?"

"Father Francis and Sister Esther were both aged and withered trees in the Lord's forest. They can now receive their just reward."

"If hot lead and a broken neck are the reward, I am not sure I want to be saved."

"You most likely won't have to worry about it. There are many gates to heaven but we enter but by one."

"I should have known better." He mumbled more to himself than to the nun. He was a lone wolf, used to his own company. He would like to just ride away but he couldn't. He couldn't just leave her.

"You should have known better than to do what?"

"To get involved."

"You are just full of Christian kindness aren't you?"

"I'll get you to your adobe mission but that's it." His words were cold, crisp and uncaring.

"Can you follow tracks?" She asked as they mounted. Bona on Buck and Sister Teresa on Sandy, the best of the horses. A burro was packed with their supplies. They turned the other two horses loose hoping they would find a good home or that someone in need would find them.

"Sure. But why would I want to?"

"I must get the crucifix. If it's the last thing I do, I must get the crucifix back."

"It very well could be the last thing you ever do. How much is it worth?"

"The gold is worth a good deal but the true value to the Church makes it priceless."

"Well, there's not much law in these parts and by the time you find some, they will be long gone."

"This is something I must do."

"You?" His voice was marked with scorn.

"The Lord will provide a way. I am not as helpless as you may think."

Leaning over studying the ground he led the way. "Their trail leads into Jornado Del Muerto."

"Journey of death?"

"It is the area between the Rio Grande and the Guadalupe Mountains." They were leaving the valley of the river and soon the sand was baked hard. Lizards shot like brown streaks of magic across the barren ocean of sand. Distance was deceiving in the desert. This colorful land, almost red in color, was vast, wild and becoming more uncomfortable by the minute.

A sand ridge curved by the wind with its crest ribbed made the going slow. Long shadows crept down the slope ahead of them. Soon the sun would be high overhead and even the animals that live in this Hell hole would hunt for shade. A white winged dove flew to a saguaro cactus. The flower would give it both food and moisture. A rabbit darted to the shade of a nearby cactus.

"Sir." She called to Bona. "May I see your revolver?

Bona stopped Buck. Puzzled by her request, He drew his Colt and handed it to her butt first.

She thumbed back the hammer, the large revolver looked even larger in her small hand. She took aim at the rabbit hiding in the shade a good twenty yards ahead of them. The weapon bucked in her hand and the rabbit flipped over backwards, the greater portion of his head missing.

"We are out of meat." She leaned over and handed Bona his Colt.

"I'm impressed. Where did you learn to shoot like that?"

"I wasn't born in a convent, my father taught me to hunt and fish as well as to read and write." As she spoke, she remembered the incredible void her father's death had caused. The emptiness, would be etched in her heart and mind forever.

Chapter Two

Jeb Fowler had been the personal trouble shooter for Grant during the war. Doing everything from espionage to courting rich ladies. Jeb did his job well, maybe too well. He was on his way to tell President Grant that his private secretary was involved in illegal activates when he was shot from ambush.

Jeb and Fran were father and daughter but they were also each other's best friend. Jeb didn't treat her like a boy or girl but like a young person. He taught her to hunt, fish, trap and ride. He also taught her which fork to use, she learned to cook and mend as well as to read and write.

She looked out the dirty second story window of her room and wondered when he would get home. She didn't know what he was working on, she only knew that it was about finished and they could have a real home, settle down and raise horses. Jeb had saved up some money and he had given President Grant his notice.

The next morning Fran walked out onto the porch of the boarding house. A stumpy white haired man she had seen around the boarding house was reading the morning paper. In a grandfatherly way he looked up and spoke to her. "Ah lass, your father was a good man. I am so sorry for your loss."

She never dreamed this could happen. She thought her father would always be there. They had such dreams, he was so important to her. She never thought about death until she was forced to do so. A creeping feeling that she was alone knocked at her heart. A void built up in her long before the official word came.

There were only a handful of people at the graveside. "Ashes to ashes, dust to dust, The Lord is my shepherd......" The words seemed to come from the morning fog hanging over the Potomac River. A clap of loud thunder seemed to give a haunting punctuation to the words of the priest. Fran had never felt anything like this. The lump in her throat made it impossible for her to even cry.

Looking from face to face she could not find a single person she knew. There was no one she could turn to. She was alone. Her first thought as they began to fill the grave with dirt was to join her father. What did she have to live for? What could she do without her father? A pain tore at her heart, a pain she didn't know if she could handle.

Her father had always taught her to fight. Fight until the opponent was destroyed by whatever means necessary and for however long it took. How do you fight what you can't see? How do you fight injustice?

The same belief that would take her father to the Lord's bosom in the hereafter made Fran choose life. The road from the graveyard led Fran to the nunnery of the Roman Catholic Church. Fran Fowler became Sister Teresa.

Chapter Three

Bonaparte Kingsley, a freckle-faced lad with black hair and blue-gray eyes curled up by the fire to sleep out the storm. But sleep would not come, his thoughts were with a milk white Arab stallion. An Arabian with a mane and tail like silk in the wind. He had often seen the mighty horse lift his head high in a proud gesture, his nostrils flaring as he raced to greet him.

But tonight the horse was down. Laying on his side with his nose stretched straight. His hair was dry, eyes closed and sealed shut with dried mucus. A deep groan came with each breath. His breathing was worse and Bonaparte knew he may not last the night.

Bonaparte had done everything he knew to do. He gave the horse steaming meal but he did not want to eat. A large lump had formed under his jaw.

"Strangles," the boy said aloud. A quick slash of his knife and yellow mucus ran from the great horse's jaw.

His father hated weakness and held violent contempt for helplessness of any kind. A hard disciplinarian that Bonaparte obeyed without question. It never occurred Bonaparte to disobey, he would be skinned alive. Bonaparte worked from sun up to dark thirty in his father's livery. Horses and barn had to be clean and neat. If there was one dirty stall, one horse that had not been groomed, he would feel his father's wrath.

Bonaparte feared what his father would say and do when he came home and found his prize Arab stallion near death. He could not leave the horse as long as there was a chance to save the animal. But he didn't know what else he could do.

Horses talk with their ears. He had learned that early in life. He could tell how they felt by the way their ears pointed. If they were back the horse was angry or fearful. They would be forward when anxious, curious, or pleased. Sometimes they would be stiff and at other times they would be lax and sagging. The Arab seemed to be telling him it was time to abandon the crazy thought he could be saved.

Blood pounded in the boy's brain, he wanted to cry but he couldn't. His throat was in the grip of a steel trap. Bonaparte put the horse's head on lap, the Arab's legs began to convulse and his body began to shake with a death spasm. It was over. Bonaparte brushed the foretop and bending down he kissed his friend goodbye.

His father would be furious and Bonaparte was almost at the stage to stand up to him. He could not take a beating for something he could not prevent and he could not hit his father.

The wind was blowing fiercely out of the northwest driving rain and sleet against the barn door as Bonaparte walked out. He carried a gunny sack with everything he owned. Holding his hat so it wouldn't blow away he turned the corner of the barn and walked with the wind at his back toward town.

He had little trouble convincing the man he was old enough to enlist and fight for the cause of the confederacy. Bonaparte Kingsley, became Bona King.

Chapter Four

The unique couple followed the tracks north. It was the shortest route to the mission and Bona thought the breeze coming from the mountains would cover the tracks with sand before long. For the time being he would pacify his feisty traveling companion.

It was near midday and the desert was barren. It would suddenly come to life in the cool of the evening. The quail and dove, which take a drink before going to roost, would be the first to the water holes. The mule deer, bighorn sheep, coyotes, bobcats, foxes, skunks all would make their way to the nearest water hole. By watching the flight of the birds or following the tracks of the larger animals, a man could find water. Water and life were synchronous in the desert.

The breeze picked up and tiny specks of sand stung his face causing him to pull his banana up over his nose and pull his hat down as low as possible. He glanced at Sister Teresa and saw that she too had covered her face.

They were crossing a barren flat, Bona could see broken terrain ahead and off to their left. It could offer shelter from the pending storm. The wind began to roar down from the mountains, driving before it great clouds heavily laden with sand. He tied the lead rope of the burro to his saddle horn and reached back and got one of the reins of her horse. He pulled the horse in closer to Buck, it would give them a little protection. The horses wanted to turn their tails to the storm and drift with it. The sand was drifting, becoming deeper and more difficult for the horses and burro. They were only a half mile or so from shelter. A half mile that could be the difference between life and death.

The burro stumbled but Buck pulled him to his feet and they continued on. Each step was an effort for the horses and the wind seemed to get even stronger. Bona pulled Buck up and the big horse turned his head away from the wind. Bona pulled a shirt out of his saddle bag and covered Bucks eyes and ears with it. Mounted he turn Buck back into the wind and they moved forward. With no sand blowing in his eyes and ears Buck broke the trail toward shelter. He trusted the hands and knees of Bona to direct him.

Sister Teresa had to turn her head to breathe. The storm increased at times to such a degree that she could not see Bona. The sand cut unbearably. The wind was a loud doleful howl in her ears. Bona couldn't see, he had to trust his sense of direction. If his instinct was not correct they would die in the storm. The horses and burro could not go much further.

Just when he thought he had missed the broken terrain he had seen earlier it was right in front of them. Over the years a shale and sandstone ridge had been formed. They were fortunate to find it. It was not a cave but an overhand of three or four feet. It was a wind break of eight to ten feet high.

They both spit out sand and the horses blew air through their noses and shook their heads. Sister Teresa took a drink from Bona's canteen. Bona took the water bag off the burro and poured some in his hat for the animals to drink.

"You got us through," she said in a weak voice.

"We were lucky, I thought we had missed it." His voice raspy with sand.

"You made our luck."

"You sure the good Lord didn't have his hand in it?" He asked sarcastically.

"No, I'm not. I do believe he heard my prayers but he needed a strong man to carry them out. What do you think?"

Bona didn't reply. He didn't let on that he too was praying. He took another sip of water, leaned back and began to fashion himself a smoke. There was even sand in his Bull Durham sack and the brown papers he took from the watch packet of his pants. He found a sulfur match and striking it to flame on his boot he lit his cigarette.

The sky was a murky gray, visibility zero. The wind seemed to be blowing harder than before if that were possible. Sand sifted over the top of the ridge, falling to the ground at their feet. They were imprisoned until the storm passed.

Sister Teresa rested on her bedroll, humming softly a tune she remembered from her youth. Fate had thrust her into this fearful circumstance. She watched her storm bound companion adjust to the conditions. Deep inside, she was afraid of him. More than once she had men undress her with their eyes, their look was enough to make her want to bathe in strong soap and really hot water. But she had not seen any evidence of this in his looks or actions. The situation was shockingly improper and yet there was something about it that made it more of an adventure and less sinister.

"Where are we?" She took a sip of water from the canteen knowing how valuable it was.

"Should be in New Mexico, just east of Las Cruces." He didn't look up as he spoke. Finishing his smoke, he crushed the butt into the sand,

"The law in Las Cruces may help me recover the crucifix" she said hopefully.

"From what I have heard, the law in Las Cruces could be helping to melt it down."

"Impossible!" She snapped. "The Lord would never allow that to happen."

"Like he didn't allow it to be taken?" Bona chucked, he leaned back into a more comfortable position and pulled his hat down over his eyes. "Better get some rest, time will pass faster."

She knew this was heathen territory and special means would have to be used to help her battle evil. She would do what had to be done to the best of her abilities. She prayed silently for strength and courage. She thanked the Lord for this man and asked that he bless him and his actions. Soon, like Bona she was asleep.

Religion had played an important part in Bona's early life. As a child he studied the scriptures and attended Sunday school. Born of God fearing parents, he learned the virtues of living a Christian life. The death of his mother, the death of the Arab stallion and the violence of the Civil War caused him to drift away from his early teachings.

Almost every experience Bona endured seemed to contribute to a worldly denial of all things spiritual. The war had been pure Hell. The horrors of combat, the shadow of death always hanging in the air. Billows of fire swallowed up dream after dream. Mangled bodies, the ruins of a great plantation or city. Rifles belching fire and death. All these things spread an emptiness through him. Made him hard, feeling little emotion or sympathy for others. One hammering blow after another changed him to worry only about his survival.

The wind went down with the sun and the mercury dropped. The cold night air sent a chill through the dozing prisoners of the storm. The sky was filled with clouds that floated one after another across the face of the full moon.

Bona had dug the makings from his pocket and was rolling a smoke when Sister Teresa woke up.

"Can we be on our way?" Her voice raspy from sleep and sand.

"Soon as I get the horses saddled and you get these bed rolls packed up."

"We have to find those men before they melt down the crucifix." She was beating the sand from her habit.

"We? You got gall. What the Hell makes you think I will help you?"

"I will find a way with or without your help!" There was an intangible strength in her that appealed to Bona.

"You going to just walk up to them and ask them to give it back?"

"First I have to find them. When I do, I will view the situation and figure out a way." She didn't speak with brashness but her words did sound confident.

"I hope you find it that easy." Bona let Buck have his head and the big horse picked his way around the cactus and underbrush. Sister Teresa followed with her horse and the burro.

Presently they came to a natural hollow with trees and water. Bona could see sign where animals and birds came to drink. You could learn much from the inhabitants of this country. If they drank here, the water must be good.

They enjoyed the rabbit roasted over the open fire and biscuits with hot coffee to wash it down. While they ate the horses and burro grazed on the herbage growing near the waterhole.

"You determined to do this?"

"Look. I confess to a degree of fear but don't think for a minute that I lack resolution."

"Well the first thing you need to understand is not to count on any help. From me or the law." Bona swore silently. He lived by his wits and off the land. He had not taken a job since the war and had no intention of doing so. He craved for the smell of a bar, the feel of a deck of cards and the excitement of running a bluff. Anyone could play four aces but it took skill to win with an inferior hand. To make a bold bet and watch men fold winning hands.

Another part of him felt a commitment to this nun and her crucifix. He had the feeling that she guided him with some magic power. She had rattled on and on about the crucifix and the children until he felt he knew them. It was crazy to try and help her, it was like drawing to an inside straight. He was smarter than that. He would get her to a safe place and turn her loose.

Just before dawn, they topped a ridge and looked down on a camp. Marshmallow clouds soft as down-filled pillows filled the pale sky. The sun just a faint glow in the eastern sky gave enough light for them to see clearly. A lone sentry leaned against a sandstone wall while several slept near a dying fire.

"That could be them!" She was excited at the thought.

"Well after viewing the situation, do you have a plan figured out how to get your crucifix?

She didn't answer. She reasoned that one man and a nun could not take on a gang of murdering bandits. But Bona was plotting to do just that. He knew that if they were to try anything, it was best to do it right away. If this were war he would open fire with his Henry and kill them in their sleep. But he couldn't do that with her watching. He didn't like the odds but had to admit he had gone up against greater and lived to tell about it.

The sentry, rifle on his knees, appeared to be napping. Bona dismounted and pulled the Henry from its scabbard. He handed it to Sister Teresa. "Well Sister Courageous, you handled that rabbit but can you shoot a man if it becomes necessary?"

"They murdered Father Francis and Sister Esther didn't they?" A stubborn persistence accented her words.

"We don't know that. This could be a different bunch."

She nodded agreement, a puzzled look clouding her eyes. Bona couldn't count on any help from her. He had seen many a man fold in the pressure of battle. He had seen them freeze when it came time to squeeze the trigger. If this happened to soldiers, how could he count on a nun?

"I'm going to work my way around and come up behind the guard. You ease your way down behind that big rock and cover me with the Henry. If things go bad, jump on Buck and get out of here fast." He knew these men were accustomed to taking what they wanted. They would hang just as high for murder as they would for murder and rape.

Sister Teresa nodded her head in agreement. Bona began to circle, keeping to the cover of rocks and underbrush. Silently he disappeared from her view. He had learned to do this well in the war where failure meant death as it would here. Gradually she worked her way down the ridge. She was congratulating herself on the absence of sound when with one tentative step, her foot crunched down on a small twig. The guard heard the noise caused by her ill placed step and craned his head in her direction. His rifle came to a ready position and his eyes scanned the ridge searching for the cause of the noise. His ears strained to understand what he had heard.

With all his attention on the hillside, he was not mindful of Bona coming up behind him. Only when the cold steel of Bona's Colt touched his neck and a strong hand clamped over his mouth did he think about his back. Sharply the Colt fell just above the man's ear, his knees buckled and he slid to the ground unconscious.

Bona moved silently through the pre-dawn light toward the campfire. Sister Teresa had informed him the leader of the band was a tall thin man, with sunken cheeks, bushy eyebrows that grew together and rotten teeth. "Good looking bastard," Bona said to himself as he moved toward the sleeping men. None of the men around the fire seemed to fit the description so he picked a mealy looking hombre nearest him. With his left forearm he jerked the man to his feet. His arm under the man's chin pressing on his throat. His right hand held his Colt covering the other two.

"He's a dead man if any of you do anything foolish!" He warned in a loud clear voice.

The men snapped awake and looked the situation over before reaching for weapons. What they saw made them freeze. Bona' strong left arm excreted such force and pressure that the man's mouth hung open. He laboriously made an attempt to breathe.

Bona had a problem of how to get the crucifix and get out of camp without getting killed. Right now it was a standoff. They couldn't move or do anything and neither could he. The answer to his problem came from a flash of fire and the crack of the Henry. The top to their coffeepot jumped into the air spinning wildly. It was what Bona needed to gain complete control.

"Spread eagle on the ground, hands in the middle of your backs."

Bona released his hold on the man and he dropped to the ground gasping for air. Quickly he pulled their revolvers and tied their hands with the ropes from their bedrolls. But the crucifix was not to be found.

Bona did find a five hundred dollar bill in one of their saddlebags. A wanted poster. Charlie Brunner, wanted dead or alive and a reward of five hundred dollars.

Bona jerked him to his feet and released his hands. With the nose of his Colt he pushed him toward the horses. "Saddle your bronc and remember this reward is for dead or alive and I don't care much which way it is."

Once the man was in the saddle, Bona tied his hands to the saddle horn and released the other horses to slow down pursuit.

Photo by Sarah

Bona lead the man's horse to where Sister Teresa waited. She knew he had not found the crucifix and couldn't understand why he was taking this man prisoner.

"No crucifix, but this one's worth five hundred dollars."

"You? A Goddamn nun?" He would have said more but the look on Bona's face and Sister Teresa swinging the Henry to point at his chest made him think he had already said too much.

Mounted, the trio started for Las Cruces. The well-worn trail seemed to wind lazily over the desert floor. With the sun coming up at their backs they plodded on. Sister Teresa on Sandy and the burro led the column, Bona was in the rear. The burro let out a loud bray of protest when the path turned sharply to climb a sage choked ridge. But a tug from Sandy made the obstinate beast lunge forward. Long ears flopping the burro trudged along.

The false-fronted buildings of Las Cruces were in need of paint and repair. This could have been anyone of the many towns

Bona wandered through. A cluster of weathered buildings, most of them strung out in a single line along the unshaded main street.

From the balcony of one, a young pretty Mexican girl leaned over, watching the strange trio pass. Her blouse half off her shoulders, with large breasts swelling out at them. Her face full of promise as she blew a kiss toward Bona.

Sister Teresa turned to see Bona give the shapely woman a nod. She let her eyes drift to the face of their prisoner. The Lord had made few uglier. His eyes were also on the dark haired girl but there was no return look of promise for him.

Their animals lined up at the wooden water trough in front of the livery. They all wanted to drink more than what was good for them, so after a few sips, Bona forced their heads up. The water slobbered from their lips dry from exposure to wind and sun.

The hostler appeared at the door. Hair and mustache so gray they looked almost white. His pants were tucked into the tops of his run-down boots. His hat held in place with a piece of rawhide. He spat a string of tobacco juice at a cat laying by the door as he made a careful examination of the strangers.

"What can I do for you folks?" His eyes were now fixed on their prisoner.

"Animals could use some hay and grain." From the stable a flurry of odors greeted them. Harness and tack hung on the wall, sacks of oats piled in a corner, a stall filled with fresh-cut hay, a few stalls that needed to be mucked, all blended into a stream of aroma that stirred memories for Bona. "Got a lawmen here?"

"Sure do." The man picked up a bucket and began to fill it with grain. "You a lawman?"

"Nope." Bona untied the man's hands from the saddle horn and none too gently he helped him to the ground. "We got a wanted man here to turn over to your law."

"Bounty hunter?" The old-timer spat before adding, "Should have been here earlier. A group went through that makes this jasper look like a choirboy."

"Was one of them tall, thin, with sunken cheeks and bushy eyebrows? Long greasy hair and rotten teeth?" Sister Teresa asked anxiously.

"Sure was." The hostler's eyes asked the question why.

"He killed a priest and him or one of the others killed a Nun, we are after them."

"They didn't stay long. Wanted to know where they could find a smelt. I sent them north to the eastern slopes. Nearest smelter I know of is in Leadville or Cripple Creek." He took Sandy and disappeared into the stable. She followed with the burro asking question after question.

Bona gave Buck another sip of water thinking about how he would spend the night.

Chapter Five

Sister Teresa was almost finished with her breakfast when Bona entered the hotel dining room. All eyes were on them as he took a chair at her table. They were the talk of the town. A Catholic nun and a bounty hunter alone together on the desert. With a little imagination the story grew and grew. To make things even more interesting, it was obvious that the nun was young and shapely. Even her flowing black habit could not conceal this from prying eyes.

"Ever feel like an animal in a zoo?"

"You don't like being a celebrity?"

"No!" she snapped.

"Well I have some good news for you."

"Good news will be very welcome."

"You are two hundred and fifty dollars richer this morning. We can pick up the reward money at the bank when it opens."

The waitress came for his order. It was the girl from the balcony. She was wearing the same low-cut blouse. With a seductive voice she asked.

"What can I get for you this morning?"

"I'll have some eggs, biscuits, bacon, and either grits or potatoes." She put a cup of hot coffee in front of Bona and poured Sister Teresa a second cup. Her eyes and attention on Bona. He had shaved, put on a clean shirt, and even combed his hair.

"Was she as friendly last night as she is this morning?"

"Aren't you just Sister Nosey?" He sipped his coffee not bothering to answer her question

The waitress came with his breakfast and rubbed her body against him as best she could. "Can I get anything else for you?" She said as honey flavored as possible.

"Maybe some coffee later." She nodded her head and with a swish of her skirt she was gone.

"Seems as if you are quite a celebrity yourself." She said with a knowing smile.

"Look. I will eat breakfast with you. I will split the reward money with you. But I won't take any damn preaching." He didn't even look up as he attacked the food. Neither spoke as Bona ate. The food was good. He thought of the reward money, it had come at a good time. It hadn't worked out so bad after all, now if he could just find a safe place to dump this bossy nun.

"We need some supplies. I understand supplies cost a small fortune in the mining towns." She sipped her coffee.

"What? You mean to say you are planning to go after those men?"

"I told you that I had to do whatever was necessary to get the crucifix back."

"Does that include getting killed? You heard what the hostler said about that bunch."

"I know but I must stop them before they melt it down."

"If they so much as spot you, you're dead."

"They will be looking for a nun."

"What the Hell do you think you are?" He spoke too loud and every head in the place turned toward their table. As he looked around the room, eyes dropped and heads turned. The embarrassing moment passed and conversation at the tables became normal.

"Yes, I am a nun. But I do not have to dress like one." She waited for that to sink in before going on. "I now have money to buy some new clothes, without my habit they will not recognize me."

"Can you do that? I mean can you take off your habit?"

"Bona I will do whatever is necessary to stop them. Nothing is more important to me that the return of the crucifix." After a short pause, she added, "Except my Lord and he will understand."

"Let me get this straight. You plan to dress like a housewife, go to a mining camp. Find these killers, turn them over to the law and get your crucifix back. Is that your plan?"

"Something like that."

"That's crazy. You were lucky once, the next time you could end up as entertainment for the whole gang."

"If you are so worried, you could always go along and protect me."

"I'm no nursemaid."

"Did I ask you to? Didn't I prove to you that I can take care of myself?"

Bona finished his coffee just as the girl came with a fresh pot. He held out his cup and Sister Teresa put her hand over hers to show she had enough.

"What do you plan to do with your share of the reward money?"

"I plan to head up north and relieve some of those miners of their gold dust."

"You can lose money at the poker table as well as win it." Bona didn't say anything so she went on. "If you are going north, we can travel together."

"It is crazy for you to even think of going." He said with annoyance.

"The golden crucifix is very special to the mission. Our people are poor and so is the mission. Onion soup is often our main source of nutrition. We do not have enough books, the only thing we have a bountiful supply of is orphan children. This crucifix is a symbol, a very important symbol to the mission and the people. I must do everything in my power to get it back. The reward money will help greatly and I will spend some of it to get the crucifix." The day to day struggle for existence of the children showed in her eyes as she spoke.

"Let's go to the bank and get the money." With a look of exasperation on his face, Bona put a tip on the table and went to the counter to pay their bill. His thoughts were of how he could get himself rid of this nun. She made him feel uneasy. There was something about her. His head was so full of conflicting demands he was beginning to get a headache. He didn't want to be responsible for anyone but himself. He liked to live day to day, with nothing to worry about and no one to care for. She seemed to have a spell over him. One adventure with her was enough.

Chapter Six

The wagon loaded with flour, a bag of beans, a bag of rice, sugar, salt, calico, denim and a variety of canned goods headed down Main Street. The burro was tied to the tailgate. She had traded Sandy and some money for the wagon and a team of horses. The team was cow-hocked with ewe necks, a poor excuse for horses but the boys at the mission would love them.

Bona watched from the boardwalk in front of the saloon. After they picked up the reward he had gone to find a game of chance. She went and bought out the general store.

Seated on the spring seat, she snapped the reins over the backs of the horses and almost got them to trot. Bona couldn't believe how different she looked. She wore a flowered blue and white print dress with a mantilla draped over her shoulders. She was right, they would never recognize her. With this new look, she was also without the protection of her black habit.

Watching her leave, he felt guilty. He was concerned about her safety but he wasn't her protector. What she planned was crazy. She had been so sure that he would ride out of town with her. St. Anthony's mission was in the valley between the Rio Grande and Pecos rivers. The Texas to Denver cattle drives had gone up the valley, the mission would often end up with the weak and played-out cattle that could not keep up with the herd. But with the coming of the railroads it was cheaper and easier to drive the herds to a railhead in Kansas and ship the cattle to Denver. Thus the mission lost their supply of beef and the poor became poorer.

The Lincoln County War caused the Pecos to boil. If you were good with a rifle, the wages were three dollars a day compared to a dollar a day for a regular cowhand. A wild, untamed unfenced land. A paradise for those with a passion for living by the gun.

The land held many different kinds of danger. Roving bands of Indians. Apaches and Navahos, war was a business to them. Mexican vaqueros. Drifters from the Civil War. All dry for whiskey and starved for the company of a white woman. This was the land Sister Teresa traveled alone. The wagon load of supplies as valuable as gold.

Bona mounted his buckskin and followed the tracks of her wagon. Rolling hills punctuated at intervals by isolated sandstone bluffs. Off to the north lay the dark purplish shapes that rose tier on tier. These were dissected by canyons and ravines. It was rugged land and no place for a woman alone. It was bad enough for a woman to travel with an armed escort.

Bona let Buck have his head he wanted to close the distance. The more he thought about her the more enraged he became. On ahead he could see the dust from her wagon. If he could see it, so could others. He cussed himself and her. This was crazy.

The burning red ball of fire pushed across the cloudless sky. Sweat streamed down his forehead into his eyes. It ran down his back, his clean shirt was soaked. The hair on the back of his neck and some sixth sense told him to hurry. He put his heels to Buck and pulled his Henry. He had learned to rely on this feeling, it had saved his life a time or two during the war.

His eyes scanned the rocky trail ahead. As he topped the crest of a ridge he spotted the wagon. Three men had it stopped. Two were going over the load of booty, the third a giant savage of a man, had hold of the team by the bridle of one of the horses. Heavy shell-studded belts crossed his massive barrel chest. He had the brutal characteristic look of a savage animal.

For a moment Bona considered calling out, but the thought was lost as the Henry came to his shoulder. Buck closed the distance quickly. The man on the wagon was the first to see Bona and the first to die. He reached for his revolver but the rifle roared before he could draw and he was flung backward before the others heard the report of the shot. Again the Henry cracked and the huge barbarian's face contorted in a horrible grimace as he staggered under the impact of the slug. Bona fired again and again the slugs drummed into his chest.

The third man did not want any part of the Henry. He turned tail and rode as hard as he could to get out of range. Bona sent a warning shot in his direction that seemed to make his horse gain speed.

Bona pulled Buck to a sliding stop and hit the ground on the run. The savage was still alive. His fingers covered his chest wounds. Blood oozing through his fingers and staining the sand scarlet. He made an attempt to speak, blood bubbled from the corners of his mouth and the only sound he made was animalistic.

Bona tied Buck and one of their horses behind the wagon with the burro, pushed the dead man off the wagon and climbed aboard. Sister Teresa sat very straight and still on the spring seat. Her eyes met his without seeming to see. Fear of the situation still showed on her face.

"It's Okay," he said soft and reassuring. He wanted to say and do more but he didn't know what he should do or say. She was sobbing. He didn't even know if she heard or understood what he said. She uttered something but it was gibberish, he couldn't make heads or tails out of it. He adjusted her mantilla and took up the reins. She dug her fingers into his arm and leaned her head on his shoulder. She was still sobbing.

Bona didn't like being on the wagon but he really didn't have a choice. The sun slid behind the rugged western horizon. Just a deep red glow filled the sky and purple shadows began to creep in as the daylight faded. Soon the temperature would drop. The sobbing was less and she appeared to be asleep. A sudden jolt of the wagon brought her back to the here and now. She released her hold on his arm and lifted her head from his shoulder. She was embarrassed.

"I didn't think you were going to save me," she said weakly. She gained a little composure and slide over on the seat, away from Bona.

"Here I was just getting accustomed to your head on my shoulder."

His ironic tone irritated her, she couldn't help the way she felt the fear had been overwhelming. It was an experience she would not soon forget. "Did you kill those men?

"Yes and no, one of them high tailed it when he found out it wasn't all fun and games." He drove in silence wanting so bad to tell her now stupid she had been. He also wanted to ask her what happened to Sister Courageous and I can take care of myself but instead he drove in tight-lipped silence.

A massive structure of sun-dried adobe brick appeared in the dim light. A stone wall surrounded the mission. A few dim lights could be seen in several windows. A gate with a large cross above it was the only way in.

"Stop here please. If I go in, Mother Superior will make me stay."

"And that's precisely what you should do."

"No!" She spoke with determination. "I am going on."

"Didn't you learn anything today?" There was a touch of anger in his question.

Her face was still white, almost ashen but now with anger a little color began to return to her cheeks. "Very well, get off. Take your horse and be on your way." She jerked the reins from his hands, eyes and head turned away from him.

Slowly Bona got down off the wagon. He stood on the ground looking up but she would not even glance his direction. She sat stiff unseeing and unhearing.

Bona shrugged his shoulders and turned to get Buck. He mounted and rode to the front of the wagon. She had not moved a muscle. "You okay?"

"I'm fine." She assured him but her voice sounded like an echo.

"You are doing the right thing. It may not seem like it now, but later you will realize...." Bona did not finish, her face was like a zombie. The reins slack in her hands the horses began to more forward toward the gate of the mission. He watched as they disappeared from his line of sight.

Chapter Seven

The pale blue light of morning seemed drab as his senses were dulled from overuse. He had rode north from the mission toward the eastern slopes of the Sierras. He was still tired he had not slept long. A large black cloud swallowed the sun in the eastern sky. Thunder rolled and re-echoed in the distance. Another clap of thunder and a flash of lightning told Bona he better get out of this low land and find cover. A flash flood could come roaring down what minutes before was a dry wash.

He quickly packed his things and mounted Buck. He took the first trail he saw that climbed to higher ground. It was rock-strewn and Buck climbed with caution. Another clap of thunder and the deluge began. A steady soaking rain that fell straight down. He was glad that he had put on his slicker before mounting Buck. The trail was grueling and becoming slippery. One slip and they could end up on the rocks a hundred feet below. Bona swung in the saddle to study his back trail and what he saw made his gut twinge.

The falling rain made it difficult to see but far below he could make out a horse and burro. They didn't take the trail he used, they were riding down a dry wash, it was easy riding and the climb was gentle but soon it would be a rushing river.

He turned Buck, swearing and cursing as he did. Why him? He thought she had given in to quick but he didn't think she would follow on her own after the ordeal yesterday. Now she was about to get them both washed away.

He pulled his Henry and stopped Buck on the crest of a ridge. Far below he aimed at Sister Teresa, her horse and burro. It would take too long for him to ride down. He squeezed the trigger and the rifle jumped in his hands. He waited and Sister Teresa pulled up her horse and looked up. The slug ricocheted off a rock just a few feet ahead of her.

Bona motioned for her to turn around as he started down the trail he had just climbed minutes before. Even in that short amount of time the rain on the trail made a difference. Buck moved with caution as the footing was not as secure as it had been.

A trickle of water started to run down the dry wash. Bona searched for a safe area of retreat. He forced Buck to a faster pace, they didn't have much time. As he rounded a bend to meet Sister Teresa he looked up and saw a little used trail. It was astonishing the speed the trickle of water was growing, soon it would be a rushing current.

Buck was hesitant he didn't like the trail but Bona's heel in his flank told the big horse he should climb. Bona had the rein of her horse and the burro was tied behind. Sister Teresa gabbed the saddle horn with both hands. It was slippery and treacherous but they gained height with each lunge. The rain made it difficult to see but suddenly Buck turned toward the rock wall of the mountain. The rain stopped pounding down on Bona, it was a cave. It proved to be huge, twice the room they needed.

Bona couldn't believe it, he would have missed it. He dismounted and stripped the saddles off Buck and Sister Teresa's mount. Fire wood was provided by a former occupant and soon a blaze lit up the shelter. Neither spoke. Each waiting for the other.

Bona rolled a smoke while she prepared hot coffee and something to eat. He noticed her dress, it was wet and clung to her body. He had to remember she was a nun. Even if she was stubborn, mule headed, half-witted and stupid, she was still a nun. He added some wood to the fire and poured himself a cup of coffee.

"I am surprised you found this haven in the rain."

"I didn't, Buck found it." He said in a curt impolite way.

"Look. I am grateful for your help. This makes the third time you have saved me. But you don't own me. You can't tell me what to do, what to think or how to act." She handed him a tin plate of food. They ate in silence. Bona was too disgusted to enjoy the meal. He ate without tasting it. His mind was clouded with emotion. He was beginning to hate this woman, this nun.

She put down her plate, turned her back and knelt to pray. "Oh Holy Mary, Queen of virgins...." She was completely absorbed with her prayer. Her voice was soft, gentle. Bona couldn't hear much of what she said but it was soothing. The fire was behind her, leaving her in shadow.

"God must look down on us and smile. To say the least we are an unorthodox pair," Bona said softly to himself. He finished his smoke and made them each a bed on opposite sides of the fire. Outside, thunder rolled, the water wagon rumbled over the bridge and the rain fell in a downpour. He added some wood to the fire, they were warm, dry and safe for the moment. He barely closed his eyes and he was asleep.

Finished with her penance, Sister Teresa washed the tin plates and cups in the water funning off the cave entrance. She refilled the coffee pot and placed it by the fire before going to her bedroll. She was exhausted, both mentally and physically, too much so to sleep. She tossed repeatedly, twisting and turning sleeplessly. Impossible as it seemed, she knew she must find a way, muster the strength to go on.

It rained all night and all the next day. She tended the fire adding small amounts of wood to keep it going. Bona didn't wake up or at least he didn't change his position all day. With darkness the rain let up and the sky began to clear. Shortly, the moon was up shining in a glowing brilliance. The land was washed clean, a sweet odor of freshness filled the night air.

Bona awoke refreshed, full of renewed vigor. He hobbled the animals in front of the cave so they could graze. It was a beautiful night.

"What are you thinking?" she asked.

"That the trout would be hitting and I would like to go fishing."

"Do you like your devil-may-care life and attitude?"

"Yes. Do you like your difficult to keep vows?"

"Can we travel tonight?" She asked, changing the subject.

"The water will drop as fast as it rose. As long as we take it slow and keep to the rocky ground we should be okay.

Bona ate in silence but Sister Teresa jabbered on and on. She would ask a question and answer it herself. She seemed to never run out of things to talk about. It was a mystery to Bona how she could eat and talk without making a mess of either. It must be one of the unique things about the female. He thought if a man were doing that he would be spitting food all over the place or forget what he was talking about.

"I had a long talk with my Lord about you last night."

"You got enough to do taking care of Sister Bounty Hunter. Don't waste your time on me."

"That's true, I do find it difficult keeping my vows."

"Chastity?"

"No. I don't have any trouble with chastity," she snapped sharply.

"Well, if you do. Just let me know." Bona had trouble not laughing. He wished he could see her face but was glad she couldn't see his.

"I have a responsibility to return the crucifix to the mission. Please do not think for a moment that you being vulgar will keep me from it."

Bona didn't reply. He saddled the horses while she secured the pack on the burro. In minutes, they were on their way. He thought as he rode. He wondered if Satan was toying with his mind, or maybe God. He couldn't ignore this emotions. He hated responsibility. He was driven by his desire to do what pleased him and when it pleased him. On the other hand, he couldn't help but feel a need to see her safely back to the mission. Only then could he relax and enjoy his freedom. Only then would he be rid of this obnoxious obligation.

Chapter Eight

Hope looked like a ghost town. Dawn was just breaking and the town was still bedded down for the night. Impatiently Sister Teresa waited. Bona had put the animals in empty stalls and fed them grain and fresh hay. He was busy with brush and curry comb while they waited for the town to wake up.

Sister Teresa paced in front of the livery. Back and forth her displeasure showing with every step. Bona didn't share her anxiety. He knew one of the first men to stir would be the hostler, coming to care for the horses. He also knew that he would know if there were any strangers in town or if any had passed through. The grain they were eating would more than make up for any time they lost. He occupied himself cleaning and checking them and their equipment. A worn strap could get a person killed.

"I thought you were trained in patience?"

She didn't answer. She took out writing materials from her pack and busied herself writing a letter. It served two purposes, time went faster and she knew it was necessary to inform the mission about Father Francis and Sister Esther. She would also let them know she was working to get the crucifix. Talking to them had been out of the question when she dropped off the wagon of supplies. In a letter she could explain without hearing their objections and being they couldn't ask questions, she didn't have to explain in detail.

She missed the children. It was sad thinking about them. They had no choice, no voice in their beginning and no voice in their growing years. She wanted them to have a chance, a chance to be all they could be. Survival was about all they could think of, day to day survival. She wanted so much more for them.

She finished her letter when the hostler came around the corner. He knew the men, and yes they were here and gone. Late the afternoon before they had rode out heading north. They had a burro loaded heavy.

"That would be Satan, Father Francis's burro. Would you post this letter for me?" She asked has she handed him some money.

"Sure enough," his smile showed tobacco stained teeth.

Bona paid him for the grain and hay and saddled the horses. It was a draw if he asked Sister Teresa more question or she asked him. A lot of people passed through and the hostler had a habit of forming an estimate of who and what they were. Normally his judgement had a high degree of accuracy. But this pair had him stumped and reading the address on the letter didn't make it any easier. "Saint Anthony's Mission. Well, if that don't beat all" he said out loud as he watched them ride away. Sister Teresa didn't ride side saddle, her skirt puffed out on both sides of her horse, showing trim ankles. No one would take her for a nun.

In Roswell they learned the same thing. The riders had been there and were gone. Pulled out that morning. It was about noon, so they were a half day behind. They followed the Pecos River north toward Trinidad. By putting in a long days ride they might catch them in Trinidad. The trail was grueling as it wove its way through canyons and deep mountain gorges. Cold camp sites of Indians and whites were abundant. Twisting their way through the mountain the views were enough to take their breath away. Once Bona thought he spotted them miles ahead but when he put his telescope on them, it was nothing but bighorn sheep.

It was almost mid-night when they reached Trinidad. The place was alive with activity. The long hitch rail in front of the hotel was full of horses. Licking his lips Bona tasted a mixture of sweat and grit. Heavy black stubble covered his face. He longed for a shave so he could feel clean.

The hotel clerk eyed them up and down and then asked for their room rent in advance. Bona asked for a room on Main Street but they were all taken, they couldn't even get rooms next to each other.

A young girl brought hot water and a clean towel. Stripped to his waist, Bone washed and shaved. He beat the dust out of his shirt before putting it back on. He would take care of the horses and make a round of the town. Before leaving the hotel, he knocked on Sister Teresa's door. "It's me, Bona." He said lightly.

"Remember, when you go to bars the Devil goes with you," she warned.

"Why is it that God is always with you and the Devil is always with me?"

"I guess in your case both God and the Devil are with you," she replied with a chuckle.

"Well, hope they got money for drinks because we're all paying our own way. Keep your door locked and don't open it for anyone."

The saloons were full but Bona didn't see anyone that matched the picture he had in his mind of the men they were after. An empty chair at a poker table crew him like a magnet.

"Straight poker," the dealer, a fatherly looking man explained. "Table stakes and no checking and raising. That checking and raisin is horseshit."

Bona nodded agreement. Now he made a careful examination of the players. He studied their every gesture, their features and their characteristics. The way they placed their bets and handled their cards. A young handsome cowhand seemed to be the big loser. He was pushing the pots to try and win back his money. An older gent appeared to be the big winner. He was playing it close to his vest so as to hold on to his winnings. The other two didn't seem to worry about winning or losing. They talked business, the business of mining and hauling freight. They played the cards as they came, staying when they should fold and just calling when they should raise. Bona came to the conclusion that it would be impossible to read these two, he would have to just go with what they had showing. The other two he could read like a book after just a few hands.

"Dammit! That's horseshit. I had a straight going in and you luck out and draw a flush." The young man threw his cards in the discards.

"I think you just hit on the mystery of life." Bona said as he was gathering the cards.

"Mystery of Life? What the Hell you talking about?"

"Nothing's fair," Bona said and he put the cards down for him to cut.

"That's for sure, I busted my backside for that money and all I get is second best hands. His eyes were like a mirror to Bona as he studied his cards.

Bona gave the game his total concentration. It was refreshing, it tended to blot out all his ills. It was a release of nervous tension that was as good as eight hour of sleep. He had learned that men played the game for different reasons. Some enjoyed a sense of power over others as they played. Some the fear of losing drove them to the tables. Some were aggressive and others were passive. The aggressive players could become passive when the cards called for it but the passive players generally found it difficult to play aggressively with any degree of success.

Winning was important to Bona but there was more. The game was an outlet for him and a chance to exert dominance over opponents. The challenge of competition and an opportunity for him to successfully play the game.

Before he knew it, it was closing time. Slowly the crowd had drifted away. The bartender and swampier were beginning the task of cleaning up. "One last hand of show-down for everything I got," the young man challenged. He threw two silver dollars on the table. One by one the players anted two dollars. It was Bona's deal. He would deal five cards face up to each player. After four cards, the young cowhand was looking like the potential winner. A pair of tens. Bona had a pair of deuces. One by one he dealt the cards and the tens were holding up. The last card was his, with his thumb he lifted the corner of the card peeping to see the third deuce.

"Looks like you got yourself a winner," he said laying the deck on the table, his card still face down on top. The young man scooped up the pot, happy to have money for breakfast.

"Damn Sister Sacrifice has me soft in the head," he said softly. He picked up his money, quickly counted his winnings and pushed back his chair. It had been an enjoyable game but he was confused. He had never folded a winner before. If he was going to feel sorry for losing players he may as well give up the game. Had he really changed that much?

He would have to be careful. A man with doubts, one who hesitates could find himself in a heap of trouble. It could be the difference in living and dying. Not only for him but for Sister Teresa as well.

Only one horse remained at the hitch rail as he stepped onto the boardwalk. Hip-shod, head down dozing it waited for its master. The clay back dun appeared to belong to some hand who had loaded up on whiskey and was spending the night with one of the many women Bona had seen in the bars. Bona couldn't remember any he would have wanted to jump in bed with but a load of whiskey does strange things to a man's judgement. It can give him blind courage and it could change an old hag into the girl of his dreams.

The hotel lobby was empty as he crossed to the stairs leading up to his room. The lamps had been turned down low for the night and sounds of sleep came from the rooms as he walked down the narrow hall.

Sleeping in a bed was a luxury he was not accustomed to. He sank into the feather-tick mattress and was asleep immediately. The comfort did not lessen his awareness. He had learned from practice to distinguish between the sounds of the night and the sounds of danger. A herd of cattle could be driven down Main Street and he wouldn't notice. A boot scrape in the hall or a hammer thumbed back and he would be wide awake. Little sounds of danger released a warning device in his system that prepared him for immediate action. Tonight, this warning system was not needed.

The comfort of the bed did cause him another problem. It aroused a desire for a lady. He could sleep out under the stars without a problem but there was something very stimulating about a bed. It could be the realization that they were available. Whatever the reason, Bona had a craving and his dreams were in response to this. None of the saloon girls could match the image created by his imagination. This lady in his dreams had natural beauty and a honey flavored voice that made his name sound like the sexiest word in the English language.

Chapter Nine

Sister Teresa went to church while Bona got supplies and saddled the horses. She was feeling a need to visit her Lord's house. The sanctuary lamp broke the dim light of the vacant church like a red spark. She prayed for guidance and courage. She made her confession and expressed penitence. Walking out of the church, she had renewed strength.

Bona, led the way with Sister Teresa leading the pack burro. In case of trouble, he didn't want to be bothered with the burro. They followed the trail north toward Cripple Creek. The quartz pushed aside as waste from mining gold was found to be almost pure silver. This gave what was almost a ghost town, new life. Cripple Creek was now famous because of rich lodes of silver.

Indian trouble plagued the region with the Cheyenne and Crow fighting each other and both of them fighting the miners and mountain men who trapped for beaver. Many died in the barren wilderness where the coyotes and buzzards fed on their remains.

The narrow mountain trail opened suddenly into a lush valley with a small stream running its interior length. The stream was a blend of white rapids and calm waters. Pine trees grew along the mountain side and the sweet scent of pine drifted to them on a slight breeze. The mountain rose in a mighty challenge behind the row of pines.

Next to the stream stood a horse. The horse and its rider wore brilliant red paint. The rider on his face and body, the horse on his neck and hind quarters. The muscled arms of the man held a lance with red streamers handing from it. He used the lance to steady himself on the horse. Jet black hair reaching his shoulders covered most of his face. Both man and beast had been wounded and were slowly bleeding to death. Bona pulled his Henry from his saddle boot and raised it to his shoulder.

"No!" She yelled. "He is hurt. Let me see if I can speak his language." She jumped down from her horse and walked toward the wounded pair.

"Be careful," Bona warned.

Slowly she walked toward the horse and rider. Neither showed any sign of being aware of her. As she drew nearer the horse started to lift his head but the effort seemed to be too great and he dropped it again. Slowly she approached speaking softly as she did. She called back to Bona.

"He's unconscious, please come and help me get him down from his horse." Bona ground reined Buck and went to help. The Indian held onto his lance with a dying man's reaction. Bona had to pry it from his fingers. He dropped it to the ground and pulled the wounded brave from the back of his horse. With his hands under his shoulders, Bona drug him into the shade. Sister Teresa had gone to the stream for fresh water. Bona built a fire while she began to clean his wounds.

After the fire was going and water placed on it to heat, Bona took a look at the horse. He too had lost a lot of blood and was very weak. With some mud from the bank of the stream, Bona packed his wounds. This stopped the bleeding. He got water in his hat but the animal wouldn't drink. Using his hand Bona splashed water on the lips and nostrils of the horse.

Bona took care of their stock, hobbled her horse and the burro and let Buck loose to graze and drink from the stream. After doing what he could for the wounded horse he went to the bank of the stream. Pulling off his boots and socks he began massaging his feet in the fast moving current.

"You're going to kill fish for a mile downstream." She was still working over the wounded warrior but couldn't pass up a chance to jest.

"Hey, that's a great idea." Bona went to his saddle bag and returned with fish line and hook. Under a log he found some grub-worms and began to fish.

She worked over the still unconscious man. With limited medical supplies, she did all she could. She cleaned and covered the bleeding wounds. She covered him with a blanket. Bona had good luck, the mountain trout seemed to almost leap out of the water to get the grubs. It wasn't long and he had a nice mess of fish. Cleaning them on the bank he made them ready for the skillet. Nothing was better than fresh trout fried golden brown. He fried the firm white meat crisp enough so he could eat the tails and all.

Sister Teresa used some of the fish to make a hot broth to force feed her patient. After eating his fill of trout, Bona went to saddle the horses. She was still trying to force some broth between his teeth.

"What are you doing?" She called.

"We're wasting daylight. If you mean to catch those killers we best hit the trail."

"We can't leave now. This man can't travel and I can't leave him." Her voice was diamond hard.

"Makes me no difference." He dropped the saddle back to the ground, checked the hobbles and returned to the camp fire where he rolled a smoke.

"The brave didn't stand much of a chance, his lance against rifle slugs." Bona spoke more to make conversation than for any other reason.

"Will his horse make it?" She had done all she could for now. He could die any minute but for now he was resting.

"Hard to say." Bona turned to see that the horse had laid down. "Lost a bunch of blood. Could be bleeding inside too. If his lungs fill up, he's history."

"You think they were shot by white men?"

"Don't know. Could be the ones you are after. How long you want to wait here?" He didn't really care. It was a nice place to rest. Fishing was good and there was plenty of good grazing for the animals.

"Until he dies or is well enough to travel."

"Hey, I could care less," he spoke with a shrug of his shoulders. "I'm going to look around. Keep the Henry handy and if anyone comes or you want me, just fire a shot." He spun on his heel and ambled away, not wanting or waiting for a reply.

He took Bull Durham and papers from his shirt pocket and fashioned a cigarette as he walked. He licked it closed but did not put a match to it. The smell would announce his presence verticality the length of the valley.

Downstream several hundred yards he found a village of prairie dogs. Slowly and silently he worked his way to a stump and watched the busy town. A young pup wobbled toward him unaware of any danger. Thinking Bona's boot was a smooth rock, the little pup sat down on the toe.

Soon they were both startled by a loud whistle. The little guy's mother sounded the alarm. The pup raced to his mother where he was chastised for wandering away.

Walking back under the pine trees, he picked up wood for the fire. The thick needles of the pines seemed to silence the wind. The carpet of dead needles under the trees would make a comfortable bed, it was like walking on a sponge.

Bona checked the horses and burro.

Photo by Ken

e lit his cigarette still hanging from the corner of his mouth. He would have a smoke and take a nap. If he didn't, she would rattle on and on about the mission or ask endless questions of his past. The only way he had found to keep her still was to make a remark about her shapely legs, her doe eyes, or her hair. She'd give him a nasty look and clam-up.

Bona had to chuckle thinking about it. What a nuisance a conscience could be. They were thrown together, miles from the nearest settlement. He wondered what it would be like if neither had a conscience. He dreamed about it.

Bona took her in his arms, she snuggled more than she struggled. He touched her soft hair and kissed her gently on the corner of her mouth. She didn't push away. His big hands held her cheeks, again he kissed her softly on the mouth. This time there was a hint of her returning his kiss.

"You are making this very difficult for me," she said as his hands went down her back to her buttocks. Her hands went under his coat as she put her arms around him. Her head lay against the dull thud of his heart. "You think I am awful don't you? You think I'm wild and bad." She whispered, her mouth against his chest.

"I think you're sweet, desirable. A rare jewel to love and cherish." She burrowed herself to him, her embrace was passionate.

The banging of a spoon on the iron skillet snapped Bona awake. The dream was so vivid he felt an awkwardness and wondered if he had talked in his sleep. The coolness of the stream washed away some of his embarrassment as he splashed water on his face.

Chapter Ten

Bona made a travois, using two long poles and a blanket. He lasted the poles to the saddle of Sister Teresa's horse. With her help he placed the wounded warrior on the sled.

"What about his horse?"

"I don't know if he will make it or not but his best chance is right here. He has water and good grazing." Bona mounted Buck and took the lead rope of the burro. She mounted and they started off down the valley. Her horse didn't know if he liked the sled that drug behind but after a mile or so he settle down.

"Must have been hitched sometime," Bona said but it was lost in the wind and noise of travel before it reached the ears of Sister Teresa. They had lost two days and the travois would slow them down. Bona had wanted to leave the Indian but as usual, she won out. It was easier to give in then it was to argue with her. Bona swore he would get rid or her at his first opportunity.

Between sign language and the small amount of Cheyenne she knew, she had been able to communicate with Traveling Bull. He and his people had come from the land of many lakes. Forced out by white settlers and soldiers. They were constantly at war with the Crow but had made a treaty with the Kiowa and Arapahoe against the white man. His small band had taken to the high ground. He and three other braves were on their way to raid a Crow encampment when they were ambushed by four white men. The others were killed.

A Rocky Mountain Jay swooped down to snatch up something from the trail ahead of them. The Jay was called, Camp Robber by most. They would steal any loose article they could carry. Anything with a shine or gleam was what they liked best.

The motion of the travois started Traveling Bull's wounds to bleed again. He was fighting for breath, struggling to remain conscious. The primitive sled was the best form of transportation they could devise but he was in no condition to travel.

Bona scanned the rocky country ahead for any sign of danger. A silver gray lobo loped swiftly ahead of them. A superb runner he would circle around waiting for a chance to earn a meal. He had smelled the fresh blood oozing from the Indian's wounds. Tonight his coarse howl would gather the pack for the night's kill. For the time being he would keep his distance. He never made a sound running and could be seen only when he didn't care.

The soft breeze flapped Sister Teresa's skirt as the trio worked higher and higher in the rough and beautiful mountains. Wild flowers carpeted the banks of sweet tasting streams. Nature had carved a design out of marigolds, blue flag and golden lady slippers. They stopped only long enough for them all to drink and for her to check the man's wounds.

"Why do men do that?"

"Do what?" Bona was busy filling his canteen with fresh water.

"War. Why do they make war on each other?"

"I can't explain war. War is like falling off a cliff. You can't stop or change direction and you know sooner or later you're going to get hurt or killed."

"I guess I can understand fighting for a cause."

"You better, because you're doing it." He took a deep drag on his cigarette before adding. "The name of the game is survival. It's teaching or learning. You either teach a lesson or you learn a lesson."

"You make it sound so matter of fact."

"Let's get this Indian to his people so we can get on with this war of yours," he said with a chuckle.

Another hour of riding and the rocky trail opened onto a high plateau that revealed the shapes of tepees toward the far end. Smoke drifted up from the smoke holes near the top. From one of the most colorful painted lodges came a young bronzed beauty. She was still in her early teens. Her black hair, large black eyes were accented by high cheekbones and firm young breasts. Bona couldn't help but notice the beauty of the young Indian girls and the ugliness of the old squaws.

Everywhere he looked, women were working. Women were cooking, hanging meat to dry, and scraping skins. There was a noticeable lack of young men in camp. The young beauty ran to the travois and spoke to Traveling Bull. After a moment or two she got to her feet and returned to the colorful tepee. She appeared with a beautiful buffalo robe, trimmed with the fur of a silver wolf. This she handed to Sister Teresa. At the same time she asked them to eat at their campfire.

Food stored in rawhide cases was prepared for them. Berries and wild plums. Tender jerked meat and pinon nuts. The camp had come to life, everyone came to watch them eat. Bona picked at his food and was a little embarrassed when Sister Teresa spoke sarcastically to him.

"What's the matter, you too nice to eat dog meat?" The Cheyenne relished dog and served it as an honor to guests. They preferred buffalo, elk and bear for grease and fur. The white man's beef was their last choice. They would rather steal a horse from the Crow and eat it than a long horn steer.

Bona ate and had to admit it tasted very good. But he did not like the admiring looks from a couple toothless squaws that had lost their men and were looking for someone to take their place. Sister Teresa enjoyed seeing him feel awkward it wasn't often that she felt comfortable and he felt uneasy.

Chapter Eleven

Cripple Creek was a hub of activity. It was still early but the street was crowded with miners and trappers. Most of the business places were tents on a wood frame. Only a few permanent frame buildings with false fronts lined the street. One of these was the livery on the edge of town and the blacksmith shop next door. The jail was the lone log building. It had iron bars on both the windows and door.

From a tent that served both as a café and bar, the smell of coffee and meat frying drifted to Bona. He noticed the sign in large letters above the door. "PAY IN ADVANCE", he wondered if that was the name of the place as well as its policy.

"We need to replace some shoes on these horses," Bona said as he pulled up to the hitch rail in front of the blacksmith shop. As he entered the blacksmith shop a burly man wearing a heavy leather apron was chewing out a young lad. Bona didn't say anything until the man quit talking and began to use physical punishment. The smith delivered a smashing backhand blow to the boy's mouth and blood spurted from split lips. Swearing loudly he placed a brutal kick to the boys ribs. He stepped forward to kick again.

"Don't do it!" Bona warned. "Just back off," Bona drew his Colt and stepped between the boy and this outraged disciplinarian.

"Damn you! You got no Damn call to..." The man stepped forward as he spoke but never got to finish his sentence. Bona hit him with his Colt right behind his ear. The blacksmith dropped to his knees and fell forward on his face. Bona holstered his Colt and helped the boy to his feet.

"Now he will kill you," the boy warned between bloody lips that were already starting to swell.

"He has to wake up first," he helped the boy to the water bucket hanging on the wall. "What was that all about?"

"One of the buggy horses is missing a shoe and I didn't see it when I put him away last night." The boy, about twelve, took a drink of the water and spit it and blood on the floor.

"My horses need some new shoes, get me some iron while I fire-up the forge." Bona using the bellows heated up the fire. The glowing embers in the forge made the iron white hot. With tongs, he took the iron to the anvil and with a large hammer began to fashion the iron into shoes. While he was doing this, the boy pulled the worn shoes off the horses. Bona liked the sound of the hammer as it struck the iron on the anvil. The ring of hot iron had always sent a chill through him. In no time he had changed raw iron into perfect shoes. With a rasp he shortened the toe and checked the angle of each hoof. No two horses are the same. Buck didn't need much adjustment but the horse Sister Teresa was riding was bad-footed. He had to do a little extra to get him shod right. He had put shoes on Buck so many times he could tell at the anvil if the shoe would fit.

Bona had a light hammer in his hand when Sister Teresa warned him that the smith was coming around. He had just finished putting on the last shoe. The boy was taking the horses outside. Years ago in his father's livery he had learned to throw a hammer with accuracy. Many a rat had been killed by a thrown hammer. The hammer was a good weapon but it didn't put fear in a man like the business end of a Colt.

The big man staggered to the water bucket and poured a dipper full on the back of his neck. He drank half of the next dipper and poured the rest over his head. He turned threateningly toward Bona. "Now you're going to die!"

"If you want some more step right in." Bona still held the hammer shoulder high, the man hesitated.

"I owe you for eight shoes I put on our horses. How much you got to have?"

"Huh! Eight shoes? Couple bucks." The smith didn't know what to make of this stranger. He wasn't in the habit of dodging a fight but his head still had a ring in it from their first encounter. He did not want to appear a coward but there weren't any of his friends around and he didn't want to invite more trouble from this stranger with the cold gray eyes.

Bona placed two silver dollars on the anvil and put the hammer beside them. Slowly he drew his Colt and leveled it on the smith. Backing toward the door Bona offered a last bit of advice.

"Next time you have to discipline the boy remember that knot behind your ear."

Outside Sister Teresa was waiting with the horses. As Bona mounted she gave his a piece of her mind. "Did you have to do that? Just because he was acting like an animal was no reason for you to act like one."

"I did not act like an animal. If I were an animal our relationship would be much different. Now either keep your preaching to yourself or find a new protector." He didn't look at her but he heard a gasp.

They rode up the rutty street, it was easier than walking as there were no boardwalks. People were coming and going. Wagons, mules, packhorses and some with everything they owned on their backs. Bona pulled up in front of the general store.

"Get what supplies we need. We can't stay in town, the only hotel is a tent filled with cots." He took the reins of her horse.

"Don't need much. I am out of Sulphur, used what we had on Traveling Bull." She got down and went in the store while Bona watched the parade of people passing.

It wasn't long before she came out, dressed in riding breeches and shirt. She even had boots that came almost to her knees. The few supplies she did have she packed on the burro. Because Bona didn't remark about her change of clothes, she felt obligated to.

"Don't know why I didn't buy something like this in the first place."

Bona didn't reply, he turned Buck away from the hitch rail and headed back toward the livery. As they passed the blacksmith shop he was ready for anything but the smith was busy and didn't even look up. At the livery they learned the men were here or at least had been yet last night. They had asked about the smelter and who the owned it.

They learned the smelter was located on the northern edge of town, away from traffic. They found it guarded like Fort Knox. It was built into the sheer cliff of the mountain between the river and the mountain. A heavy guarded bridge was the only way in or out. Some of the ore came down the river but wagon loads of it crossed the bridge. The guards checked every wagon and every person wanting to enter.

Bona asked one of the guards if anyone answering the description of the men they were after had checked in. He was told that two men with a burro had been there but were not allowed to cross. The men had asked a bunch of questions and returned to town with the burro.

"Is there anyone else around that could melt down a large hunk of gold?" Bona rolled a smoke while he spoke.

"The blacksmith. He could cut it up and melt it down in small pieces." The guard seemed puzzled by the question.

"Did they ask for any information?" Bona put a fire to his cigarette.

"Funny thing is, they asked the same as you."

Bona drew the smoke into his lungs with a deep drag. He thanked the guard and turned Buck back toward town and Sister Teresa. She was full of questions. Bona was silent. He was thinking. Somehow they had to keep an eye on the blacksmith shop. He couldn't leave Sister Teresa alone and he couldn't stay in town with her. For all he knew, the men could have moved on or they could have made a deal with his friend the blacksmith. It was a chinch he wouldn't get any answers from the smith.

The answer to his problem came in the form of the boy the blacksmith had abused. Bona saw him walking toward them. The boy recognized him and waved a greeting. Bona pulled Buck to a halt by the young lad.

"Hello, are you okay?"

"Yeah thanks to you."

"Wonder, if you could help us?"

"Be glad to, what can I do?" The boy had a puzzled look on his face as he looked up at Bona.

"We're looking for some men who stole a large golden cross and we think they will try to get the smith to melt it down for them. They were in town yesterday, four men with a burro."

"They were at the shop and I heard them tell Mac they would see him tonight." The boy's eyes shone with pride at being able to help.

"Do you know where they went?"

"Rode out of town east, had the burro with 'em."

"Where can we camp nearby where we won't be bothered?"

"You can stay at the cabin. My Uncle Ben's cabin. It's just outside of town on the river. Uncle Ben is gone and won't be back for several days. Come on, I'll show you." The boy started off toward the river.

"Here, climb up." Bona kicked his foot out of the stirrup. He couldn't lift his foot high enough to reach the stirrup, so Bona reached down and swung him up behind him. In just minutes they were at a tar paper shack. It was as dirty a rat's nest as Bona had ever seen. Built of tar paper, canvas and sticks. It looked like the first good wind would blow it into the river. Even the flap used as a door was all shredded to pieces. The only good thing about the place was that it was out of the way and yet near town. It was also on high ground so with his spyglass Bona cold see most of Main Street.

"I'll care for your horses," the boy offered jumping to the ground.

"Thanks. Just put the saddles here," he pointed to a log beside the shack. "Give 'em a good drink and hobble that horse and the burro, the buckskin don't need hobbles." He handed the boy the hobble ropes from his saddlebag.

Not wanting to go in the smelly shack, Sister Teresa began to prepare a meal outside. Behind the cabin was a nice level slab of rock that overlooked the river. Before long they were all eating and visiting like they had known each other for years. The boy, Tommy Burns, asked almost as many questions and talked almost as much as Sister Teresa.

His mother had died last winter. She had been a camp follower, sleeping most of the day and gone most of the night. Tommy was left to make his own existence the best he could. Only heaven knows who his father was. Tommy at the age of ten had seen enough to curl the hair of most temperance workers. He had been exposed to gambling, sex, violence, profane language and the ways of mining camps, he had the makings of someone tough as nails or someone who dies at a young age.

"Your uncle, what's his name?"

"He's not my real uncle, he was living with mom when she died and he said he would look after me." The boy was lean, wiry with black hair and eyes. He was quick to smile and both Sister Teresa and Bona took an instant likely to him and he to them.

"And does he?"

"Does he what?"

"Does he take care of you?"

"Well, it lets me live here."

Sister Teresa, her knees drawn up to her chin, sat on the stone wall looking down on the river. Her thoughts drifted from Tommy to the children at St. Anthony's. They were so much alike in so many ways. "Just pray and believe...."

"And do!" Bona interrupted. "Don't forget to do." He was enjoying a smoke and the fact that he really did not have to talk unless he wanted to.

"Yes, you have to do too. It's okay to believe in miracles but you have to do your part". Tommy looked at her and smiled. He wasn't sure what she was talking about but he liked these people. They were very different from the mining camp inhabitants. Oh Bona looked like some of the men but he didn't talk or act like them.

"Tommy, could you scout around. Check out the town and see if you can find any sign of the men we are after?"

"Sure. I can go anywhere and no one ever even sees me." He started to get up, "Want I should shake a leg right back here if I spot 'em?"

"Yes, and be careful," Bona warned. He cleaned and oiled his guns while Sister Teresa went down to the river and washed the tin plates and herself as well. After washing her face, arms and hair she felt much better. She wished she could jump in and take a swim. The water was clean as it was upstream from town and almost cold, it was very refreshing. She could see Bona checking the saddles and equipment. From where he was on the bluff, you could see for a mile or more in both directions. She took her time combing out her hair. She looked up again, this time he was watching her.

Chapter Twelve

Bona King was in trouble. Trouble was not new to him but this sort of trouble he had little experience with. This woman, this Sister, seemed to be able to talk him into anything. On top of that, she never did anything he told her to do.

He had told her to wait with Tommy that he would check out the blacksmith shop. Now here she was, her and the kid. The gambling joints and bars were doing a land-office business, the hitch rails were full. The noise covered his movements. Kerosene lanterns did a fair job of lighting Main Street but behind the shops, it was dark as a blacksnake's back. Bona had to feel his way, pausing often to listen. He could hear voices coming from the shop. Light shone through cracks in the large back door.

With an eye to a crack he surveyed the shop. He could see several men and the smith who had his back to him. They stood around something on the work bench. All of a sudden the smith slammed down his hammer and swore.

"No damn it! You dirty sons of Satan want me to do your work, I get an equal share."

"Bullshit!" The skinny, pale faced killer replied. "You get what we agreed on. No more and no less. Now get started." He shifted the rifle he carried from one arm to the other.

"You guys need me. It's worth an equal share and I mean to have it."

"All we need is your equipment. Keep bitching and you're a dead man."

Bona waited, his eyes slowly sweeping the scene before him. They were ready to kill the smith and undoubtedly would after he did what they wanted. It had always been his habit never to interfere when his enemies were destroying themselves, so he waited. When and if he did take action, he wanted to be swift and totally unexpected. Bona didn't mind a face to face battle but he sure didn't like the idea of having a woman and kid behind him to catch a wild shot.

He checked the door, it opened out but was latched on the inside with a bar. He would have to go around front or find another way in. His mind raced. He should be feeling some fear, he should be concerned about the odds but he wasn't. Adrenaline raced through him causing him to seek action.

The smith was coming to the same conclusion as Bona. He had himself between a rock and a hard spot. He knew they could very well kill him, it was only a matter of when.

"Okay, you win, but this has to be done right. It will take time." He knew he was backed into a corner and he needed time to figure a way out. A large lamp with a round mirror behind it shone down on the golden crucifix. He worked the bellows pumping air into the forge, heating the coals white hot.

"Keep working the bellows while I get things ready," the smith handed the bellows to one of the men.

Bona had worked his way around the shop and was at the front door, his Colt leveled. His voice cold and cutting broke the silence. "Don't move! Lock your fingers over your hats." He thumbed back the hammer of his Colt to let them know he was ready and willing to put it into action. He was in the shadows and they were all under the light of the over head lamp.

"Slow and easy now, turn around." Slowly they turned but they could not see him in the darkness of the shop. Bona didn't like the nervous eyes of the man on his left. His eye lids barely parted, his opaque black eyes glinted with anger and curiosity. His fingers like a claw over his hat seemed to twitch with itchiness.

Bona was about to speak when the man on his left, the one with the nervous eyes went for his holstered gun. It was a move of self-destruction. Bona's colt spoke death before he even cleared leather. His body slammed back into the wall, the force of the man's body making the lamp sway on the shelf. Bona shifted his attention to the others as the lamp fell to the floor.

The kerosene spread over the warn floor boards and leaped into flames. The men scrambled in panic. "He shot Carlos!" One of them yelled in the confusion. The smith seemed to forget how near he had been to death. An iron hard fist caught Bona just under the heart and sent him flying back into a rocking chair. It was splintered into fire wood as Bona rolled to regain his feet. The smith charged and Bona smashed his Colt down over his head for the second time that day.

Bona could feel the heat of the fire on his face and feel it in his lungs when he took a breath. He had to drag the smith outside or he would burn to death. Tommy was yelling to him from the door. "Bona! Bona, you okay?"

Bona drug the smith by his heels to the middle of the street. As he was doing this he could hear people yelling a warning of fire. People were coming with buckets of water to put out the fire. Fire was greatly feared as the town was mostly tents.

"Tommy, jump into that saddle," Bona pointed to a horse still tied to the hitch rail. It must have belonged to the dead man, the other two had taken off with the cross, leaving the burro and the dead man's horse.

Sister Teresa was on her horse and held Buck. Bona grabbed the lead rope of the burro and vaulted into Buck's saddle. He turned Buck away from the crowd coming down the street and they disappeared around the corner of the burning shop.

He led the way, keeping to the cover of darkness. At the edge of town, they turned onto the only road leading out of town to the west. The road followed the river, winding up into the mountains to the northwest. For several miles there was only one possible way the men could go. The river had cut a deep gorge in the rock and sheer cliffs lined the other side of the river and the side of the road they were following. Bona didn't know now far it went like this but for the time being he didn't have to worry about reading sign or an ambush. But as the road climbed and curved an ambush became a greater worry. These killers had shot an unarmed priest so they wouldn't hesitate shooting from ambush.

He now had a woman and a young boy to take care of. It still made him angry the ease with which she influenced his judgement. Like with Tommy. It only took her a few minutes to get him to agree to bring Tommy with them. He had to admit the mining camp and that dirty shack was no place for the boy but he wasn't sure being in his company was much better.

"Let's pull up for a minute." Bona wanted to collect his thoughts. He turned Buck off the road and dismounted by the river.

"Did you kill one of them?"

"He didn't give me any choice."

"Was he the one who killed Father Francis and Sister Esther?"

"No. He is still ahead of us with the crucifix." Bona went to the river for a drink of water his throat still felt dry and parched by the fire.

"Why are we waiting?"

"Want them to think no one is following. Push them too hard and they will shoot us from the rocks. Tommy, you better shorten your stirrups."

"Where do you think they will go?" Tommy was busy with the stirrup leather but he was never too busy to ask a question.

"Leadville, Fairplay, hard to tell. They could turn east to Denver. That's what I would do if I were them." Bona reloaded his Colt.

"Why would you go to Denver?" Tommy had finished adjusting his saddle.

"More chance of selling the gold, either as is or melted down."

"True, not just everyone would have enough money to buy it even if they wanted to, in Denver they would have a better chance to unload it." Sister Teresa cupped her hands and took a drink of water from the river.

"How long do you plan to wait?" Tommy was as antsy as Sister Teresa.

"Long enough to convince them they got away clean. We should eat something, once we start to travel we may not have time to eat."

Sister Teresa nodded her head in agreement and went to the saddlebags for jerky and cold biscuits. They ate without speaking, the noise of the river and the howl of a wolf added back ground music for their meal. To the east and down in the valley they could see the glow of the blacksmith shop. It would burn most of the night and longer if some of the tents caught fire from the sparks.

Chapter Thirteen

T he river and road had been cliff bound all the way but now it opened into a deep canyon with several smaller canyons running off it like fingers of a hand. Bona dismounted and searched the ground for sign.

"I've lost their sign," he took out the makings from his shirt pocket and began to fashion a cigarette.

"Where are we?" Sister Teresa had been unusually quiet.

"Just south and east of Leadville. They could have gone on west to Leadville or turned back east to Fairplay or Denver." He put a match to his smoke and took a deep drag.

"What do you think we should do?"

"I've a hunch about Denver. They didn't have much luck in the mining camps."

"I think we should follow your intuition.' She paused a moment and then added, "How far is it to Denver?"

"About twenty miles to Fairplay and a good hundred from there to Denver."

"Is Fairplay out of our way?"

"No." Bona crushed the butt of his smoke under the heel of his boot and mounted Buck. A few minutes later a flock of prairie chickens rewarded them with two birds. Bona skinned and gutted the birds, cut off their heads and feet and washed them in the cold mountain stream.

"Build a little fire, put these on a spit and roast them golden brown," he handed the birds to Tommy.

"We going to camp here tonight?" Tommy asked as he gathered wood for a fire.

"No, just eat and rest the horses. We'll go on into Fairplay after dark." He pulled the saddles off the horses, rubbed them down with a handful of grass and hobbled them to graze. He didn't hobble Buck, he wouldn't go far and would come to his whistle. The other two would run off the first chance they got, so he was careful with their hobbles.

He watched Sister Teresa and Tommy fix supper. She was only a little over five feet tall and weighed no more than a hundred and ten or fifteen pounds. She was tender, yet she was tough. She was frail, yet she was strong. She was small but she was imposing. She never ceased to amaze him. Her determination was no surprise, with her it was never could it be or might be, it was absolute. He couldn't understand the power she held over him. She had him doing things he never dreamed of doing.

After they had eaten they sat silently around the small fire. Bona was enjoying his after dinner smoke. Sister Teresa, with her knees drawn up under her chin, stared into the fire. Tommy was licking up the last of the chicken.

"Just like a regular family," Tommy said smiling from ear to ear.

"What?" Bona questioned.

"We're just like a regular family," he repeated.

"An orphan, a nun, and a drifter don't make a regular family. Get the horses saddled".

The hurt showed in Tommy's face, he so wanted to be a part of a regular family but he jumped to his feet to do as he was told. As he did he asked, "Isn't this what regular family members do?" He didn't wait for an answer, he went to do as he was told.

"He's not your enemy, you don't have to be so ugly." Sister Teresa got busy packing things away. "You tend to push people away if they began to care about you." The light from the fire made her eyes shine like the green eyes of a cat.

"I don't want him planning things, he may not like the ending." He stood slowly. "The best of plans can be made but accidents tend to control the outcome."

"True but humans are social animals, they have a need for each other and Tommy needs somebody, somebody to care about him."

"He best not bet on a nun and a drifter."

"Drifters only drift until they find something worth setting down for." She was smiling but Bona wasn't.

Bona whistled for Buck and moved away into the darkness. She had a way of making him feel very uncomfortable. To her life was so simple, but he knew it could be very complicated. It could be very cruel. It was not always fair and the good people didn't always live happily ever after. She had great pride. Pride could be an evil growth. Pride could get you killed for nothing. You add a dash of stubbornness and a cause and you got a bad mixture.

"I have a feeling we're quarreling about something but I don't know what." Bona pretended not to hear. He knew he couldn't win a battle of words with her and he didn't want to get angry. When he was angry he couldn't concentrate on the dangers of the road. Anger was not a luxury he could afford, like pride and cause it could get you killed.

Chapter Fourteen

Fairplay, an inviting name, Bona thought as they entered town. He remembered what mining camps were like and he doubted the name fit. It was larger, more people with more problems than Cripple Creek. Horses stood with their heads down at the hitch rails. Shadows spilled across the dusty street. Light came from dirty windows or tent flap openings into the street. Noise from the gambling tables filled the otherwise quiet night.

Bona wanted to take a quick look around but he didn't know what to do with his traveling companions. It was a chinch he couldn't take them with him. He looked around for a safe place to leave them, if there was such a place in a mining town. As if in answer, to his wish, he saw a cross about the opening of a tent set back from the street. He turned Buck toward this temporary house of the Lord.

A kerosene lantern lite the dim interior of the church. Crude wooden benches on the dirt floor. A rough likeness of a pulpit stood on a platform at the front. It wasn't much but it was a place to hold a worship service. It was more than most mining camps had.

"Wait for me here," Bone instructed and turned without another word and went out.

He went from saloon to saloon looking for the two men. Most of the places were packed to the rafters with miners. In his rush to cover the town as quickly as possible, he ran into a snag. In the turmoil of a place known as the Greasy Spoon, he ran into a working girl. She was one of the most repulsive women he had ever seen. She grabbed his arm, her mouth reaching for his neck. Her hands walked up and down his chest and back. Without thinking he pushed her away. Several days and nights of too much to drink made her unsteady on her feet. The push caused her to lose her balance and fall in a heap on the dirt floor of the saloon.

"Why you son-of-a-bitch, who do you think you are?" She was almost to her feet when she slipped and fell again. Bona reached out to help her up but she kicked his hand away.

"Get the Hell away. You think you're too damn good for the likes of me?" Her scream was like the warning slap of a beaver's tail on a mountain pond. The whole saloon became conscious of the incident.

Bona shrugged his shoulders and turned to leave but the hand of her drunken friend clamped down like a vice on his shoulder. With a jerk he spun Bona around to face him.

"Ya apologize." The drunk demanded in an insolent tone of voice.

"Sure, whatever you say," Bona couldn't help but grin. "Peg pardon madam." Almost immediately he wished he had been more sincere. If he had, maybe the drunk would have let it drop.

"Don't ya make fun of me!" He was pushing fifty, over weight and soft. His face a pale deathly white under several days' growth of gray stubble. He had been drinking courage all day and wanted to impress his friends. A more sober man would have turned away from Bona's steady clear-eyed stare and the feel of his muscular shoulder when he grabbed him. But the man was too drunk and he had backed himself into a corner. He had gone too far, said too much, to let it drop.

"Make the saddle tramp pay," the woman spat. Once she may have been pretty but the years had been hard and had taken their toll.

Bona dropped his left hand to the butt of his Colt and made a quick draw. He jammed the barrel into the man's belly up to the cylinder. The drunk lost all his good air and his lungs burned to replace it. Bona removed the Colt and let the man gasping laboriously for air look into the bore. His thumb worked the hammer. The sound had a sobering effect on all those looking at the barrel of his Colt.

The weapon had done what words could not accomplish. The dispute was settled. Had Bona just hit him with his fist a real donnybrook, a free-for-all would have broken out. There were few things these men liked more than a good barroom brawl.

Slowly, Bona backed out of the saloon. As the swinging doors closed behind him the hush that had fallen returned to the normal sounds of drinking and gambling. He moved sideways away from the saloon and crossed the street. He didn't holster the Colt until he mounted the steps of the church.

The scene inside the church was directly opposite of the one inside the saloon. Alcohol, games of chance, violence and wanton women were replaced with a picturesque scene of a woman and your lad kneeling in the flickering light of a burning candle and the kerosene lantern. It was difficult for Bona to understand what a huge difference a hundred yards could make. This view was so calm so serene, it was free from anything sinister. What was even more difficult for him to understand was how he seemed to fit into either of these two extreme situations. A moment ago he could have been in a barroom fight and now he could join the two kneeling before their Lord. Who was he, was he a stranger even to himself?

Chapter Fifteen

Dust covered them like dried salt water. A fine white powder made them look like they had been riding drag on a cattle drive. After a swim in the fresh mountain stream and a hot meal they were refreshed. Riding all night and all day, they had covered much of the distance to Denver. Tommy was bushed, with his swim and the hot meal in his tummy he dropped off to sleep before Bona finished his second cup of coffee and smoke.

Sister Teresa joined Bona by the stream. The grass on the bank was as soft and thick as a wool blanket. The stream spoke the language of love as it rippled over the rocks. As natural as taking a breath, their faces turned and Bona kissed her warm lips.

"No!" she twisted away from him, a faint tremor in her voice as she protested his advance. "Please, don't do that."

"Damn woman, I'm only human." Without her habit she unleashed an earthquake in his body. He savored the smell of her.

"I'm sorry. We can't do that." Her eyes were filled with tears as she spoke.

"I've never wanted anyone like I want you."

"That's just it, you want me. You don't love me and anyway I have given myself to my Lord."

"Love?" He hesitated. "I don't know as I even understand the feeling of love. I do understand want and I know I want you."

"Want is just a need, a desire. Love is a devotion. A tenderness that is unselfish. It is to cherish." Her voice was muffled by his arm. Bona had to strain to hear. He could feel her breast against his chest. Blood pounded in his temples, a wildness inside him was hungrily seeking to be satisfied.

She pushed to get away. He could feel a swelling in him like a sea pent up with energy. He wanted the pleasure that only a woman could give a man. He knew he could take her and for a moment he considered it. He had never forced himself on any woman and he was not about to start with her. She pushed harder and rolled away from him. He stared up at the stars and moon not knowing what to say or do. The stars seemed to be tree-top high, brilliant.

"I wish I would have known you before."

"Before what?"

"Before I took my vows."

Wishing don't do any good." A bitterness edged his words.

"I'm sorry but you have to understand."

"I really don't have to understand anything. I go out of my way, risk my damn neck and what do I get?"

"You were never promised anything."

"Why did you parade yourself down here in the moonlight smelling like a woman if you're not a woman?"

"You have to understand."

"All I understand is that you drive me crazy. I couldn't bring myself to let you run off by yourself and I can't stand to be around you."

"I'm sorry but you must understand my vows. My vows mean so much to me."

"And what am I to do?"

"Go take a cold swim, smoke a cigarette and go to sleep" she spoke with a touch of a giggle which only inflamed Bona more.

He began to walk away, stopped and turned toward her. The sounds of the stream and the far-off yap of a coyote broke the silence. They gazed at each other, both feeling the frustration of the moment.

"You know I could take you if I wanted to."

"Yes but you won't. You're not the kind."

A shadow in the night sky seemed to close over them like a blanket. Tonight by this mountain stream would be etched in their minds forever. Bona watched as she got to her feet and walked back toward the campfire. The fire was just a bed of red and yellow coals glowing in the dark.

Chapter Sixteen

The look in his eyes was that of a man waiting to hear the sentence from a judge. He hoped to be set free but fearful he would be sentenced to death. Would he be fast enough to be set free or would he be second best and die on this barroom floor. All was quiet as they stared into each other's eyes looking for a sign of weakness. One would be the judge sentencing the other to pain and possible quick death. There was one other consideration they both had in the back of their minds. At this distance, it could be a tie or near enough that both could get off a shot. It was unlikely that either would miss. This could be a no win situation.

Beads of sweat began to appear on foreheads. They were at the point where anything, a slammed door, a cough a flinch would set off the chain of action that would turn the silence into a deathly shooting gallery. Both were young, healthy and strong. Seconds that seemed much longer, elapsed. Neither wanted to make the first move but both wanted to be the fastest.

If this were a fist fight, they would both try to land the first punch. Make it a good one, to gain the advantage. In a gun fight it was more final. Once the hammer fell on the charge of gun powder, death could leap into action. There was no shooting the gun out of his hand, or drawing so fast you didn't have to drop the hammer. Once the action started, one or both could be dead or dying.

The man facing Bona was stocky, short with powerful arms. A shock of jet black hair showed from under his high crowned hat with a single feather in the sweat band. The man's Mexican blood was not to be missed. He wore high moccasin boots, dark pants and a colorful shirt. His strong shoulders said he would be tough to beat in a brawl but this was a gunfight and he was facing Bona.

Seconds ticked off, the Mexican started to speak. He bit his lip and remained silent. A flicker in his eyes warned Bona that he was going to draw. The two shots were so close together they sounded almost as one. Both men seemed surprised the other had drawn so fast and without any visible effort. The air was filled with the smell of burnt gun powder.

Bona was spun around by a burning fire in his right arm pit. A light danced in his head as a warm wetness spread down his arm. The room whirled and his legs turned to jelly. He lost his balance and the floor came up to slap him in the face.

A slight difference in quickness had been with Bona. His slug turned the Mexican just enough to make his shot miss dead center. Blood oozed out of the Mexican's mouth and he choked as he made an unsuccessful effort to speak. Bona wasn't aware of any of this. Blinding flashes of pain shot through him. He fought to keep from losing consciousness. His brain clogged with thoughts of survival. With his good left arm he attempted to push himself up. His Colt still in his hand. His right arm hung as if broken. The pain caused him to stop all movement to allow it to subside.

"That's the man! That's the desperado who kidnapped my nephew." It sounded as if it came from a deep stone well. The words echoed around and around Bona's head. He fought to understand. "Now he's killed a man! Marshal do your duty and haul his butt off to jail."

The law office stepped forward and took the Colt from Bona's fingers. None to gently, he hauled him to his feet and gave him a push toward the batwing doors. The crowd of on lookers watched the winner being treated like a loser. One man, with nervous eyes in a pale thin face checked to see if he was attracting any attention as he slipped out the back door.

Bona felt the barrel of his own Colt in the small of his back. He was forced out onto the boardwalk and down the street to the Denver jail. The cell was small with very little light or ventilation. Bona sat on the edge of the rough mattress, blood dripping from his wound to the flagstone floor. Marshal Owens slammed the cell door and turned the key in the lock.

The flagstone floor gave off a hollow reverberating sound from the boot heels of the marshal as he returned to the outer office. "Jess, go get the saw-bones. That jasper needs some fixing up or he will bleed to death."

The cell was small but the odor coming from the next cell made it seem even smaller. The rank odor of urine. Bona could hear a man snoring, most likely a drunk sleeping it off. Closer inspection of his surroundings made him realize that some of the odor came from the mattress he was seated on. He noted the barred window as he ripped his shirt with his good left hand. The walls had been painted with lime and they contributed to the smell.

With every beat of his heart, his arm throbbed. The slug had missed his rib cage and the bones of his shoulder and arm. He removed his bandana and pressed it into the wound. He fought to stay alert. His mind flashed back to the saloon and the voice he heard, the voice that sounded like an echo.

"That's the man! That's the desperado who kidnapped my nephew. Now he's killed a man!" So the Mexican must have died. Kidnapping? That could only mean Tommy. Bona turned it over and over in his mind. Tommy had told them the man was not his uncle. Had Tommy lied to get out of a bad situation? He wondered how long it would take the doc to get to him. They didn't hurry too much for a man in jail. He wanted to lay down but he feared that if he did he would pass out and bleed to death. He had to keep pressure on the wound. In his mind he felt this could all to straightened out. Tommy could let them know he was not kidnapped and the fight was self-defense. The guys in the saloon would testify to that. It was just a matter of not bleeding to death before the doc got to him.

The pressure had eased the bleeding but the pain was still there. The throbbing pain and the loss of blood had him a little light headed. He wished the doc would get there and the jailer. He wished he could talk to him. Have them find Tommy and Sister Teresa. She had gone directly to the church, taking Tommy with her.

She was feeling depressed with guilt. She needed to make her confession and ask forgiveness. Kneeling beside Tommy, her hand over his. "Join me in saying, Our Father." Tommy didn't know the prayer so he did little more than mumble softly as she spoke the words. Together they lite a candle and Tommy waited while she made confession, expressed penitence and received the Sacraments.

Tommy felt some embarrassment, some confusion. In his short life he had seen and heard many things but he had no experience with church or religion. This was the first time he had ever been inside a real church. Sister Teresa went to light a taper before the Virgin Mary. "O Holy Mary...." Tommy in a pew nearby waited and watched. He didn't understand all of her words and movements but he felt something he had never felt before. She looked and sounded so at home, so peaceful in her serenity. Tommy could see and feel the joy she received. Her prayers were more than mere words. As she knelt, completely absorbed she gained strength and courage.

From the church, they went to the café where they were to meet Bona. They found a table and checked the menu on the wall behind the long counter. The sign, fly specked and stained from grease and smoke had been in place several years. The aroma coming from the kitchen made them forget the unsightly menu. The dinners all came with choice of apple or cherry pie.

Two men at the next table were talking so loud and with such arousing excitement that they couldn't help but notice. "That's about as near a tie as you'll see," the man had chin whiskers like the tuft of a Billy goat.

"Yeah, the left hander was just a hair faster." He pushed the chicken and noodles onto his folk with a hunk of bread.

"Good thing too, it was just enough to make the Mexican miss dead center." He stroked his whiskers as if to wipe it clean.

Sister Teresa lost interest in the menu as she listened with intent. Bona should be here was he the left hander they were talking about?

"He still got hit pretty good and hauled off to jail to boot." He chuckled as he spoke, "Didn't pay to win."

"What was it the man said the left hander done?"

"Kidnapped some kid, wasn't it?"

Sister Teresa and Tommy both started to speak, neither spoke but both got up to leave. The man had to be talking about Bona. He was hurt and in jail. There was no way either of them could eat until they found out what happened and if it really was Bona.

They hurried from the café to the jail. The doctor still had not been there. They found Bona seated on the bunk, holding his blood soaked bandana to his right shoulder. His head was down and his features were pale and strained. The pool at his feet seemed to widen with each drop of blood.

"Please open the door. Tommy, get some clean water and cloth." As she spoke her eyes studied the jailer, a wimp of a man behind a scared oak desk. He didn't move or show any interest in what she was asking. She didn't hesitate, from the rifle rack on the wall she pulled down a Henry and levered a shell into the chamber before pointing it at the surprised jailer.

"Open the door." Her voice had changed, the harshness made the man jump to do as she ordered. Bona looked up, a half smile on his face. If he didn't hurt so damn bad and feel so weak he would have enjoyed watching this snip of a woman get what she wanted.

"We're not in town an hour and you get yourself shot and thrown in jail." She had him flat on his back, his shirt ripped away from the wound. She jabbered as she worked. The faster she worked the faster she jabbered. "You're just like a little boy. You have to be watched every minute." She cleaned the wound and put on a clean white bandage.

"You're lucky to be alive." She finished her work and stood back to admire her nursing.

"You sound disappointed."

"Disappointed?"

"Disappointed that I am alive." He had to admit, just her being there made him feel a whole lot better. Yes, he hated to acknowledge it but this nun was special.

Chapter Seventeen

Sister Teresa talked the judge into giving her custody of Tommy and dropping the charges against Bona. With the help of Tommy she got Bona in a boarding house. He was weak from the loss of blood but the Doc said with rest he would be good as new in a few days. She had just checked Bona's wound when Tommy came running in.

"Bona! Sister!" He yelled as he bolted up the stairs. "I saw him! He's leaving town!" He almost knocked Sister Teresa down as he rushed into the room.

"Whoa boy. Slow down and tell us what you saw." Bona was propped up in bed, he held up his good left arm as a signal to stop.

"The man with the cross. I just saw him leave town." He burst out between gasping for his breath.

Bona started to rise but Sister Teresa pushed him back with a gentle but firm hand. "You stay right where you are. I will go get the marshal. Tommy, which way was he headed?" As she spoke she lifted Bona's Colt from the worn holster, concealing it from their view.

"West, he was headed out of town going west." Tommy was excited with the important news.

"If the marshal won't do anything hustle right back." Bona didn't feel well enough to argue with her.

"Tommy, you stay with Bona until I get back, I shouldn't be too long."

The mid-afternoon sun was warm as she hurried to find the marshal. As she passed the livery, she called to the hostler to saddle Buck. If she went with the marshal, she wanted a horse that could keep up.

The marshal was gone and wouldn't be back before dark. She didn't wait to hear it all but turned and hurried back to get Buck. Buck was full of energy, standing in a stall for a day and a half eating hay and grain made him want to stretch his legs. At a gallop they rode west through the streets of Denver. She was so light in comparison to Bona that Buck felt as if he was running free. Once out of town the big horse seemed to literally fly down the road.

The road would disappear gradually in the distance and suddenly reappear again as they topped a grade of rounded a curve. A few miles west of Denver as they were on top of a high hill Sister Teresa spotted a rider far ahead. She pulled Buck up to a nice smooth canter. She didn't have a plan, it had all happened so fast. She only knew she had to find a way to keep the crucifix from being carried off. Even at this slower pace she closed the ground between them. The rider didn't seem to be in a hurry nor did he seem to be worried about being followed. Maybe this rider wasn't the man she was after.

She saw him leave the main road and disappear into a stand of trees. If he were going across country she would have to keep him in sight. She put her heel to Buck and he picked up the pace. In minutes they were at the spot where he turned off the main road. She pulled Buck to a walk as they entered the trees, Buck seemed to know what they were doing.

Just a few feet into the cover of the trees, Buck came to a halt. She was about to nudge him forward when the smell of a Sulphur match came to her nostrils. She dismounted and with the big Colt in her hand she slowing inched her way from tree to tree.

"This Colt's got a hair trigger and I am real nervous so if I were you I'd get my hands up." Surprised, the man turned to face her. The cigarette hanging from the corner of his mouth. He looked Sister Teresa up and down, coldly appraising her with animal like eyes. His lips in a slight angry smile didn't seem to move as he spoke. "I thought you was a nun?"

"Never mind that. You know why I am here." She held the big revolver leveled at the center of his chest. She was proud of the fact that she caught him off guard. If it hadn't have been for Buck she would have rode right in on him and he would have the advantage. Now came the tough part, getting him and the crucifix back to Denver.

"And if I don't do as ya say? What ya going to do?" He was standing with his feet shoulder width apart thinking that he could draw and kill this woman as she would hesitate and be reluctant to act.

Without a word and moving only the tip of the barrel she squeezed the trigger of the Colt. The slug went between his legs just inches from his man parts. She thumbed the hammer back to firing position before the echo cleared the trees. His smile was gone. He maintained an outward calmness but lost the brazen look of disrespect.

"If I am forced to make a choice between killing you and losing the crucifix.....you are a dead man."

"Okay, I believe ya. It's been nothing but trouble anyway." He was thinking of a way to gain control.

"Use your left hand to reach over and with two fingers lift your gun and drop it to the ground. Be careful because I am nervous and I really would like to have another reason to kill you."

He did as he was told, his eyes never leaving hers. He was not accustomed to being disarmed, say nothing of having a nun do it. He was obviously shaken. If he ever got this woman at his mercy he would enjoy himself tremendously. He was little more than an animal and it showed.

The sun was just beginning to dip behind the tall aspens to the west. It would soon be setting behind the mountains. She hoped to be back in Denver before it was fully dark if at all possible. They were in a small valley with a steep grade to the west which made it seem later than it really was.

"Now step forward a couple steps and reach down and do the same with the knife in your boot." When he complied she spoke again. "Now move over and pick up the sack. Be careful with it. I have great respect for what's inside and very little for you." She never took her eyes off his eyes, she could see what he was doing without turning her head or moving her eyes.

"Now put the sack on that stump." Without taking her eyes off his she nodded toward a waist high stump to his left. He put the gunny sack on the stump. "Now, spread eagle, on your face." Slowly he got to his knees and then on his belly. "Spread your arms out wide and don't move, I will not hesitate to shoot you in the back."

As he did what he was told, she did her best to copy Bona's whistle, hoping that Buck would come to her. She had left him in a bunch of small pinon trees and juniper bushes.

Slowly, Buck came into view. "Good boy, come here Buck." Again she attempted to copy the whistle she had heard so often. Buck trotted up to her, she was careful not to let him get between her and the murderer of Father Francis and Sister Esther who was still flat on the ground.

Once in the saddle, the Colt still pointed at the center of his back, she moved over to the stump. The sack was almost too much for her to lift with her left hand but she managed.

"Now, slowly get to your feet and get moving."

"What about my horse? My gun and knife?"

"You're walking and you won't be needing your things." She started Buck toward him.

"But you can't just leave my things here. It's at least five miles to Denver. You don't expect me to walk all that way." He was moving as he spoke, looking back at her over his shoulder.

"Just don't do anything that will give me an excuse to shoot you, right now I am remembering how you shot Father Francis." They were only a few hundred yards from the main road. She was careful not to let Buck swing his head to the right and get in the way of her having a clean shot at his back. Mr. Sun was dipping behind the Rocky Mountains causing deep purple shadows to form.

Once on the main road to Denver she pushed him to move faster. They met a couple different riders coming from town. They drew strange looks and she was asked if she needed any help but she was quick to assure them that she was in control. Her captive was silent but continuous in his effort to slow down or find an escape route.

He didn't succeed at either and once they were near Denver a parade of people fell in behind them. Everyone was curious, eager to know what was going on. Why this woman with a gun was marching this man to Denver. They were all shouting questions at her and offering their help. One man ran ahead to get the marshal.

They were just inside the city limits when she saw the marshal riding to meet them. "What do we have here?" The people all crowed around to hear what was being said but were careful not to get between her gun and prisoner.

"He took this crucifix from Father Francis of St. Anthony's and killed him when he did it. He also killed Sister Esther at the same time." She pointed to the gunny sack.

"Where and when?"

"Several weeks ago, near the Texas and New Mexico border. There were four, he's the last one." Now the crowd had formed and was blocking the street. "Go on. Break it up." He motioned to a deputy to take the prisoner. "Get him to the jail and lock him up." He rode into the crowd and waved his arms as if he were herding sheep. "Get moving people, it's all over, nothing more to see. He looked up at Sister Teresa with a warm smile on his face. "I will need you to sign some papers. Is this something that you do often?" He didn't wait for her to respond. He took the gunny sack, and led the way to the hitch rail at the jail. He remembered her grit and determination from the day before with Bona.

"For a nun you sure have a different way of doing things."

"I guess I am a different type of nun."

"Well, if you're not careful....."

"The Lord rides with me," she interrupted.

"That could be true, but sometime the Lord may be busy with some other business when you need him most." He took the golden cross from the soiled gunny sack. "I will keep this until I check out your story. Don't leave town."

Back at the boarding house Bona sat up and listened with a frown on his face while she told her story. Tommy had a hundred questions, he wanted to know every detail. "You say Buck came to your whistle?"

"If it hadn't have been for Buck stopping when we got into the trees, I would have rode right into trouble. Buck was the real hero."

"He must have smelled the man and his horse." Bona was still frowning.

"So you see. You were wrong. With Buck's help, I can take care of myself." Bona still had a scowl but his color was improved, he had been worried sick about her and he thought she was with the Marshal. "I think you have more courage than good common sense."

"If you mean scared to death but determined, then I had courage." She pulled the blanket up around his shoulders as he laid back.

Chapter Eighteen

The Wells Fargo office was their last stop before leaving Denver. Bona and Tommy were all decked out in new outfits. Bona had new black denim pants, a blue-gray shirt and kerchief to match and what looked like a new hat but was really his old black Stetson cleaned and blocked, Tommy had a new white hat, a plaid shirt, brand new jeans and boots.

Photo by Angee

"It seems like such easy money after it is all said and done." Sister Teresa was five hundred dollars richer, Raid Pritchard, the man she turned over to the marshal had a five hundred dollar price tag on his head. So did Miguel Pyros, the loser of the gun fight, so they both were riding out of town with their pockets full of money.

"You guys are rich." Tommy was proud as a peacock just being with them.

"Not rich Tommy. In fact, you may have more than both of us. If that mine of your mother's turns out to be worth anything."

"That's all your so called uncle was after." Sister Teresa too had a new riding outfit, they were on their way to the mission but she had not put her habit back on yet.

"Cripple Creek is on our way to the mission so we can stop and check out your mine." Bona still did not have full use of his right arm so he was riding with the reins in his left hand. This was something he had never done as he always kept his left hand free to use his Colt if necessary.

"You really think the mine could be worth a lot of money?" Tommy was excited just thinking about it.

"Never can tell," Bona glanced at Sister Teresa and smiled. "An old prospector named Henry Comstock staked a claim and he came up with the Mother Lode in Nevada."

"Wow!" Tommy beamed at the thought of gold.

"Had to be a reason why he followed us to Denver and wanted you so bad." Sister Teresa was pleased that the judge had given her custody.

"You also got to remember that a thousand other prospectors just like Comstock didn't find a single nugget. It don't hurt none to dream but don't count your chickens before they're hatched."*

*This quote comes from an old 16th century fable and is attributed to Aesop.

They had no reason to hurry so Bona and Buck sat an easy pace. They weren't trying to catch anyone and no one was chasing them. All that remained was for him to get them back to the mission so he could get on with his own life. A couple hours down the road they came to an excellent camp site.

"Looks like a nice spot to catch a mess of yellow perch." A small lake was nestled between two steep bluffs. You could enter only from the north. The steep rock walls formed the east and south walls and the lake lay to the west.

Bona had as much fun watching Tommy catch fish as he did catching them himself. Tommy couldn't make up his mind if he liked catching or eating them best. He was good at doing both.

Later by the camp fire, Bona told a story about an Indian boy who camped in this very spot many years ago. Making the story up as he went, he held Tommy's attention to the point that Tommy could see himself as the Indian boy. After the story they all had another piece of cold fish before curling up in their bed rolls by the fire. Bona was the last as he had another smoke and checked the animals.

He awoke early, his arm was stiff it missed the comfortable bed at the boarding house. He decided to go for a walk and let them sleep. It was a pretty morning and he walked a greater distance than he planned. He was about to turn back when he came upon another early morning inhabitant. A large rattler, the Colt jumped in his hand and the snakes head went flying before he had time to think about what to do.

"Sorry old man, from the number of rattles you got, you been around a long time." He spoke aloud as he held the rattler up for inspection. There was a large distinctive rock with a flat side facing the trail that marked the spot. He dropped the snake by the rock and made a plan to have some fun with Tommy.

Later as they rode, he was telling Tommy how important it was to notice every detail and keep a sharp eye. "The main thing is good eyes. You have to spot danger before it can hurt you." They were still a hundred yards from the flat rock. Bona drew and fired. He hoped the slug wouldn't hit a rock and ricochet, and it didn't.

"What?" Tommy yelled.

"What are you shooting at?" Sister Teresa questioned.

"Rattler, big sidewinder that could have spooked the horses up there by that rock." He did his best to sound matter-of-fact and not laugh.

"That's too far, you can't even see a snake that far." Tommy said with a touch of sarcasm.

"Okay but you better take a look before you bet your new shirt on it."

Sister Teresa was enjoying the two. They were alike in so many ways and Tommy attempted to copy everything Bona did. He was even beginning to speak in the same slow drawl and he tipped his hat at the same cocky angle.

Tommy heeled his horse and rode ahead. Jumping off by the rock his horse shied away from the smell of the snake. He got his horse under control, searched and picked up the dead rattler his head shot clean off. His eyes were as big as horse biscuits when he turned to show them the dead snake. The horny interlocking joints at the end of the tail made a sharp rattling sound when he shook the snake. His horse jerked away ripping the reins from Tommy's hand and ran off bucking and kicking. Bona took Buck and caught the runaway. When he got back with Tommy's horse, Tommy had used his new folding knife to cut off the rattles.

"I still don't see how you did that. I just don't believe....." Tommy let it die out as he looked at Bona for an explanation.

"Like I said, you need sharp eyes and you have to spot danger before it can hurt you. You just learned not to jump off your mount and grab a snake. Had you been alone, you would be a foot right now. This is not a good place to be without your horse." His tone of voice was serious. Tommy nodded his head.

Sister Teresa rode up beside Bona and spoke softly so only he could hear. "I thought I heard a shot early this morning but was still half asleep and didn't know if it was for real or in my dreams. Now I know. Don't be too hard on Tommy, just a frown from you crushes him."

"Can't coddle him. Only the test of fire make fine steel."

"True. I am glad he has you to learn from. Teach him but be gentle if you can." She paused. "He is such a fine young man."

"What you guys whispering about?" Tommy turned in his saddle to look back at them, the question was on his face as well as his lips.

"Never mind, just lead the way and keep a sharp eye." Bona smiled when Tommy turned quickly to watch the trail ahead.

"You are his hero. It is strange and new for him to have someone to.....to share things with." She continued to speak softly so Tommy wouldn't hear.

"Great hero. I just took a man's life in Denver and almost lost mine in doing it."

"You didn't take his life. He gave it away." She paused before adding, "Tommy needs to learn when and what to fight for. I can teach him about eternal life, how to use his brains but he needs you to teach him so many things."

"You forget we are not a pair. When I get you two safely to the mission, I won't be seeing Tommy or you again." He had lost his smile. He knew Tommy should be learning how to read and write. He also knew the great adventure of war was not what the young Bonaparte Kingsley thought it would be. There had to be more to life than drifting but drifting seemed to be in his blood. It was what he liked to do.

They were at the edge of rougher country. Ahead, lay the dark purplish shapes of low bluffs. The bluffs rose, tier on tier, like great shelves. When the sun was high overhead they stopped briefly for lunch. They were on a high grassy knoll. They looked out over steep walled canyons cut into the rock years ago by rushing water. The knoll was surrounded with trees. Tall Aspen and Jupiter trees.

Sister Teresa ignored his last statement as she enjoyed the beautiful view. "This country is contagious. It would be a great adventure building a ranch on a valley like this. It would require faith and courage." She was in a trance, a state of ecstasy.

"It would take dedication and an investment in caring." Bona took out a cheroot. Sister Teresa had got him some in Denver, she liked the smell of them much better than the cigarettes he rolled.

"Bona, did you really see that snake and shoot it from that distance?" Tommy was still baffled.

"No Tommy, I didn't but it sure did look like it. Just goes to show you can't always believe your eyes. That's why you have to think with your head and trust your gut feelings. You did that and I am proud of you for questioning it." He gave Tommy a wink, a wink that said more than words.

Chapter Nineteen

At ten o'clock in the morning, not a single female was to be seen on the street of the mining town. That is, with the exception of Sister Teresa. She rode down the main drag flanked by Bona and Tommy.

The claim office, which was also the post office and law office was their first stop. They learned the location of Tommy's mine. The also learned that the ore tested had not been of high grade but good enough to work. Tommy had to sign several forms. Sister Teresa held and guided his hand as he signed his name.

"You must be the youngest mine owner in this territory." The green eye shade covered features that suggested weakness. He stood just over five feet, his frame looked to have suffered from too many years bending over maps and claim forms. His skin was pale and eyes watery. He may have looked weak but in this mining town he had power.

"So if he wants to sell, all he has to do is sign here?" Bona pointed to a line on the bottom of the claim form.

"That's it but before he sells, he should talk to the CMA boys."

"CMA?" Sister Teresa questioned.

"Colorado Mining Association. They are a big company that will work a claim for a percentage. They got an office in the back of the Golden Nugget." As he talked he shuffled papers, his eyes never meeting any of theirs.

Bona thanked him for his help and information. As they were leaving he couldn't help but wonder if the clerk got a fee for sending mine owners to the CMA. Well, it was something to think about, no harm could come from checking it out. One thing was for sure, Tommy couldn't work the mine and he wasn't about to. "I think we should ride out and look at the mine." The others agreed so they rode on toward the Lucky Lady.

Bona pulled Buck to a halt on a ridge, just out of rifle range of the mine. The bright mid-day sun caused the boiling water of the stream below to give off a mystic spray. The long slope of deep grass in front of the trio made the view something to behold. A more careful surveillance of the terrain told him the mine was occupied. He checked up and down stream for a place to ford. The water, ice cold was too strong a current to swim the horses. The rocks were water smooth and made footing for the horses a problem.

"So that's my mine?" The excitement and pride came out with each word. "Let's ride down and take a look." He couldn't wait to find gold in his very own mine.

"Hold it Tommy, somebody is working your mine and all that open ground gives them a great field of fire." Bona doubted that there was any imminent threat to them but if they went in too fast they could find a hail of hot lead coming to meet them.

"It's my mine, how can they work it?"

"No one here so they just moved in."

"Isn't that against the law?"

"Yes Tommy but there is little or no law in these parts."

Sister Teresa now saw what Bona had seen earlier. Next to the wall, near the entrance was the remains of a small fire. A thin trail of smoke still rose from the near dead ashes.

"If we ride in slow and easy like we are looking for a spot to cross the stream, I think we're safe." Bona held Buck to a reluctant walk as they rode down the long slope toward the stream. Sister Teresa and Tommy held their horses a few feet behind Buck. Bona hoped they did not know who they were or why they were here. Just three riders looking for a way to cross the rushing white water of the stream.

A tall, heavy boned man, deeply tanned by the sun and wind stepped out of the mine. Under his arm he carried an old double barreled shotgun. A film of dust covered him from head to toe. The mark of hard labor showed on his face. It was impossible to judge his age from this distance. He watched them approach and with careful intensity he noted everything about the strange trio. Their bedrolls strapped behind the cantles of their saddles, their full bulging saddlebags. Their clothes. He checked anything that would give him a clue as to who they were and what they were up to. His hands idle on the old scatter gun as another man emerged from behind him. This man was younger, holding as old sharps rifle. The old buffalo gun had the range to knock them out of their saddles, but it was only a single shot.

Bona could tell they were exchanging words but the rushing water drowned out all sound. Slowly they walked their horses forward. "Just ride easy and don't make any sudden moves," Bona spoke without turning his head. His eyes went up and down the stream checking every detail. A narrow trail lead both ways from the mine. It was crowded between the stream and the sheer rock wall of the mountain. Bona rode relaxed to with ten yards of the stream before the older of the two called a greeting.

"Hello! Looking for something or someone?" His voice carried a serious tone as it snapped like the crack of a whip at them.

"Howdy!" Bona pulled Buck to a halt. "Is there an easy ford nearby?" He leaned forward in the saddle as if to rest his backside after a long ride. Their horses showed sweat streaked flanks and faint rings of foam around their mouths. All this would tend to make them look like they were just passing through after a long ride.

"What takes you off the main trail?" A small, weathered sign caught Bona's eye. Lucky Lady. The name of the mine on Tommy's claim form. It had fallen from its place and lay against the rock wall near the opening to the mine.

"Heading to Durango, hoped to cut off a few miles." Bona paused. "If we don't find a ford it could turn out to be the long way." He sat relaxed, without the look of a man hunting trouble. He did give off a strong message that he could use the walnut handled Colt on his left hip, that he did not have any fear but that he was not looking for trouble.

"Easy ford about two miles downstream. The trail will put you back on the main road to Durango." The miner nodded downstream as he replied.

"Thanks." Bona nodded and heeled Buck into motion downstream. This was not the time to question them about mine ownership. That scatter gun would cut all three of them at this distance and Bona didn't have any reason to draw on them, at least not yet. All three had all they could do to fight the temptation to turn and look back as they rode south. The expectation of a shotgun blast went up and down their backs. Outwardly they were calm riding easy out of ear and gun range. Tommy was the first to break the silence.

"Did you see the sign? That's my mine!" His voice a challenge to why they were leaving without even a word or question to the claim jumpers.

"Yes, I saw the sign." He continued to walk Buck along the rushing flow of white water.

"Well?" Tommy raged.

Bona gave Tommy a look that told him he did not approve of his tone of voice. Farther and farther they rode from the mine. Bona rode easy checking the trail on the far side of the stream. A beaver dam a mile downstream changed the whole picture. The rapid current turned into deep quiet water that broadened out into a small lake and just below the dam was an easy crossing. Bona wondered at the works of nature. It would have been a major job for men to dam up this stream, yet beavers had done it. Even as they rode, they heard the sharp crack of a beaver tail on the water. Their signal to take cover.

"That was not the right time to tip our hand Tommy." Bona led the way into the water, stopping to let the horses take a drink and rinse out their mouths. Once on the other side he continued south following the trail. He felt sure at least one of the men would check to see if they took the trail to Durango. He wanted them to feel sure they were in no danger. Tommy never said a word as he followed over a small hill and around several sharp curves.

"We'll wait here a spell and then double back." Bona swung off Buck. He took out paper and tobacco and began to roll himself a smoke.

"You sound as if you think those two are killers. They don't look like killers to me." Tommy still sat in the saddle, his leg hooked over the saddle horn.

"What does a killer look like?" Bona asked the question but didn't wait for an answer. "Gold does funny things to honest people, say nothing to what it does to those that are a little shady to begin with."

Sister Teresa got out some jerky and sour dough biscuits for them to lunch on. As she handed some to Tommy, she agreed with what Bona had said.

"Bona is right. Just the thought of your gold mine has changed you."

"Huh. How?" Tommy bit off a hunk of jerked beef as he waited for her to explain.

"You didn't do anything to earn the mine. Yet you call it yours. You can't wait to see the first nugget of gold." Her voice carried a hint of disappointment that even Tommy couldn't miss.

"I was only thinking that.....well....if I had money." He paused and looked down, not wanting to look either of them in the eye. "If I had ah.....had money, you would want me." His voice became soft, chocked as he finished.

"Tommy, we let you come when you didn't have a penny to your name. Do you really think money would make a difference? If you could buy us, you wouldn't be happy with who we were." She gave him a light punch on the shoulder. A sign of relief escaped Tommy's compressed lips. He lifted his head and gave them both a smile. He didn't see Sister Teresa give Bona a smile and shake her head. He was back to work on the jerked beef and biscuit.

After fifteen or twenty minutes Bona mounted and they worked their way back north toward the mine. The trail veered left and right, running parallel with the stream. The bubbling sound of the rushing water covered any sound their horses made. Bona had measured the distance from the mine to the crossing in his mind. He wanted to go the last quarter mile on foot. The road made an almost right angle turn around a rock bluff obstacle, this was the land mark he was looking for. A few small trees grew in the corner and he ground reined Buck among them. Sister Teresa and Tommy wrapped their reins around small aspen trees and tied their horses.

She pulled Bona's Henry from the saddle boot and fell in step behind Bona. Her face flushed with a rush of blood from the excitement. Bona shot a glance over his shoulder and with a finger to his lips, signaled silence.

There wasn't a breath of a breeze and next to the rock wall it was very warm. Not even the cool sound of the rushing stream could lessen the discomfort. Bona led the way, making a careful surveillance of the trail ahead. He reached the conclusion earlier that they kept a lookout at the mine. The man had been right there to challenge them earlier but his field of vision did not cover this trail. Bona did not have the details of a plan in mind, only to get the drop on them without shooting if at all possible. Tommy, his eyes lit with excitement followed, being careful to hug the wall as Bona and Sister Teresa did.

They were now within fifty feet of the mine. The appetizing aroma of a pipe reached Bona's nostrils. He had smoked a pipe from time to time but it never tasted as good as it smelled when someone else puffed on one. He turned to signal the others to wait while he crept forward.

The Colt slid from its place on his left hip to his hand as he moved like a shadow. Another odor came to him, the smell of alcohol mixed with that of a work weary body. The guard was just around the corner, only inches away. Bona could hear his breathing. Even the puffs on his pipe sounded magnified.

Bona wished he knew the position of the guard. Holding his breath, he couldn't wait any longer. He had to poke his head around the corner. He hoped the man had a pipe in one hand and a bottle in the other. As he peered around the rock wall, Colt first, the first thing he saw was the back of a man's head. He sat on a folded blanket, leaning against the wall.

The cold muzzle of the Colt behind his ear and Bona's soft words made him freeze stiff. "Don't move a muscle." Bona warned as he moved forward, took the old sharps and handed it back to Tommy. He couldn't see any other weapons, but wanted to be sure.

"Stand slow and put your hands on the wall. Don't as much as twitch or you're a dead man."

"May as well kill me, if you don't Pa will." He did as he was told. Bona removed a hunting knife from his belt and an old Navy Colt from his waist band. He handed both of these to Tommy

"Who else is in the mine?"

"Just Pa." His nervous eyes showed how angry he was with himself for being so careless.

"Come here Sister." Bona spoke softly as he turned the man so his back was to Sister Teresa. "Put your rifle on his back bone and if he moves....." He let it die out as he moved forward and stood behind a heavy wooden brace at the mine entrance.

"Call your Pa out hear and no tricks."

"Pa! Hey Pa! Come out here." His voice didn't sound noticeable shaken. "I don't think he can hear," he added much softer.

"Yeah," a voice echoed back to them. "Ain't got a choice." Bona could hear the man walking toward them. Each step of his boots a hollow message of his advancement. "Damn lantern ran out of kerosene." He continued toward the waiting Bona hidden behind the brace to the mine. All he would be able to see was the silhouette of his son in the entrance of the shaft.

Bona waited. His heart pounding. Again he held his breath as the footsteps approached and passed his hiding place. The man carried his shotgun in one hand, the dead lantern and a sugar sack in the other.

"You said...."

"Just drop what you're carrying," Bona cut him short.

"Do as he says Pa, I got a rifle in my back." Now the voice was shaky with fear.

"What? What the.....?" He stammered as he dropped the things he was carrying and raised his hands shoulder high.

"Now move over into the daylight in front of your boy" Bona had his Colt in the man's back to help him do as he was told.

"Sleeping again?" He asked his son sourly.

Bona's hand on his shoulder made him halt like a soldier standing at attention. Bona's hands searched for and found a knife and pistol he removed from the miner.

"Both of you get over there and take a seat." Bona motioned toward a log near their cooking fire. He holstered his Colt and reached for a cheroot in his shirt pocket. Leaning against the wall he thumbed a match to flame and lit his smoke.

"Tommy, get the shotgun and sugar sack. Empty the gun and give me the sack." Tommy did as he was told.

"That's two weeks diggings," the man protested. Bona opened the sack and looked inside. He had seen this much gold panned out of a good stream in two weeks.

"Let me introduce you guys to the owner of the Lucky Lady." Bona turned to Tommy before adding, "Show them your claim."

Tommy took the paper from his pocket and handed it to the older man. He looked at it and gave it to his son. The boy took his time reading the paper, as he handed it back to Tommy he spoke to his father. "It's official," he gulped.

"Can't be," the older miner gasped. "We're working for a lady, fifty-fifty split."

"That lady must have been my mother."

"Must have been?" Digging into his hip pocket he came up with a plug of chewing tobacco. He bite off a corner and returned the plug to his pocket.

"Yes," Bona replied, not offering to explain.

Things were not as they had seemed. The five were silent. No one knew just what to say or do. They were confronted with the knowledge that they had a decision to make.

Chapter Twenty

Bona dismounted and ground reined Buck. He slid his rifle from the boot and moved to a position he could survey their back trail for the better of two miles.

Photo by Ken

All afternoon he had the feeling they were being watched. The hair on the back of his neck had a tingle to it. He hadn't seen a thing, but he couldn't shake the feeling. He had this same feeling several times during the war and it had always proved to be a good warning. "Take care of the horses," he spoke to Tommy without taking his eyes off the narrow trail leading down into a valley broad enough to graze a thousand head of cattle. He could be a man of patience when it was demanded of him. He sat and watched for over an hour without seeing anything out of the ordinary.

Sister Teresa brought him some lunch of jerked beef, cold beans and water. He took it and began to eat in silence. A full moon was rising in the cloudless sky, he could see almost as well as if it were daylight.

"Not much you can do with supper without a fire." She spoke more to make conversation than to explain the food.

"It'll do." Bona had his mind on the eerie feeling that something supernatural was out there. Everything looked normal. Their view was like a painting of the perfect valley to raise cattle and horses. Fresh water, lumber, grazing knee deep the length of the valley and natural fences of rack to keep the stock from drifting. If it wasn't for the spooky feeling he had of being watched, he would have enjoyed the view.

"Did you ever see a better place to build a home and start a ranch?" She sat with her arms around her knees, her shoulders hunched forward. A cool night chill seemed to ride in on the rising moon, she wished she had a blanket to put around her shoulders.

"No, and it's free land too. All you have to do is settle on it and hold it. The holding part could be tough at times." Bona wanted a smoke but he didn't want to take a chance. The flare of a match, or the glow of a cheroot could be seen for a half mile. If there was someone out there, he didn't want to give them a target to zero in on.

"Do you ever think about having a place of your own?" Her voice muffled by her arms and knees. She was drawn up in a ball like a little chimp.

Bona noticed the chill in the air as he moved behind her. He put his hands on her shoulders, gently rubbing his hands on her shoulders and back. He leaned over, smelling her hair. He could hear Tommy still working on the horses. He would brush them by the hour. Picking out their tails and manes with his fingers. Bona had never seen Buck looking better. He didn't know who enjoyed it more, Tommy or the horses.

"Sometimes, like now, you talk and act like a regular woman." His hands followed the curve of her shoulders, down her arms and across her back. Slowly, gently.

"Did Tommy do the right thing?" She asked, changing the subject to something more comfortable.

"It was good enough for his mother." Bona was more interested in her than he was her conversation. He bent down, his mouth on her hair over her ear.

"But do you think they will give Tommy his fair share?" She was warm and affectionate to a point and he had just reached that point. All at once she got to her feet and went to where Tommy was.

Bona had forgot all about the feeling of being watched. This new feeling had taken over control of his mind and body. He never would have believed he could or would do the things he was doing. It was only by chance he had become entangled but over the days and miles he had changed. He had lost his desire to gamble and seen what was waiting over the next hill. This very valley would be good enough for him. He could spend the remained of his day's right here. The land would give him everything but her. He needed her. He wanted her.

Bona couldn't understand if the reason he wanted her so bad was because he couldn't have her or if he was really infatuated with her. For a long time he sat and thought about what he wanted in life. He didn't know very much about woman, most of his experience had been with saloon girls. She was definitely not a saloon girl type. Why did life have to be so complicated?

Sister Teresa and Tommy had long ago gone to their bed rolls. He still had this feeling they were being watched but decided he was not going to learn any more tonight. He would take both his problems to bed. Sister Teresa and the ghostly feeling of being watched.

Once in his bedroll, sleep came quick and hard to Bona. He dreamed, He dreamed of a log home. Tommy was there and he had a little sister. He could only see the back of his wife. She was about to turn around when he heard a hiss....a thud.....and a groan.

These sounds were not in his dream, they were for real. He snapped awake, Colt in hand. Laying at his feet was a man with an arrow through his heart. The man still clenched his knife in dead fingers. He was only inches from putting the knife in Bona.

"What the....." Bona jumped to his feet.

"Bona?" Sister Teresa called softly. "What is it?"

"A dead man, in camp, right at my feet." He was looking out into the darkness for the man and bow who fired the lifesaving arrow.

"My debt is paid." The voice was not in English but Bona was sure he understood.

Sister Teresa held her blanket in both hands pulled up to her chin as if to protect herself. "Bona, that's the killer of Father Francis and Sister Esther."

"He must have escaped and Traveling Bull saved us." As he spoke his eyes searched the darkness.

"We thank you for our safety." Sister Teresa spoke in the native tongue of Traveling Bull while she still held her blanket up to her chin.

"What's the problem, what's going on?" Tommy was awake. He couldn't see the dead man or understand that was happening.

"It's okay Tommy, go back to sleep I will tell you all about it in the morning." He drug the man by his heels to a spot that would be his grave. From out of the night, Traveling Bull appeared. With a quick flick of his knife he removed the dead man's scalp and disappeared back into the night without a word.

Bona spent a half hour covering the body with rocks to keep the animals away and to save the others from having to look at it in the morning. He was the last. The last of Father Francis and Sister Esther's killers. Now they could rest in peace. In two days the crucifix would be in its rightful place. It would be hanging over the altar at St. Anthony's mission.

Chapter Twenty-one

"The mission never looked so good," the excitement of seeing the children was in her voice and in her eyes.

"Lots of water over the dam since we were here last." Bona pulled Buck to a stop outside the gate. "Couple times I didn't know if we would make it."

"Yes, I know. I am so happy to be back with the crucifix."

"So, what happens now?" Tommy asked.

They had not talked about what would happen once they got the crucifix back to the mission. Now, neither spoke. They exchanged looks. They both knew that once Sister Teresa was back at the mission she had her duties and vows. She knew she had to explain to her Mother Superior where she had been and what had happened. It was going to be difficult.

"I'm not staying here. I won't even go in there. If I go in that place they will keep me." Tommy turned his horse away from the gate. He rode slowly away.

"I understand how Tommy feels. I hope you understand I must do this." She had the reins of her horse in her hand, the burro was tied behind with the golden cross. "I'll meet you guy's right here in the morning, shall we say at seven o'clock?"

"Sure. You do what you have to do and we will be here in the morning." Bona watched as she led her horse into the courtyard. Soon she would be in another world, surrounded by children and their mutual attraction for the mission. This was a part of her world Bona and Tommy didn't understand and couldn't share with her.

Bona thought how complicated his life had become. It had been so easy getting sucked into the drama of this nun and Tommy. He didn't want the responsibility, the burden but he didn't like the thought of saying goodbye.

He turned Buck and put him into a lope to catch up with Tommy. He had planned to ride into town and play some poker. He had thought Tommy would stay with Sister Teresa. He was more involved than he had realized. He enjoyed watching them around camp. Both could bubble with excitement, his life was more about them than he ever dreamed it could be.

He caught Tommy and they rode side by side at a ground eating lope. The dusty New Mexico trail leaving the mission far behind them. The small village around the mission had no bar or hotel. Sister Teresa had said they could stay at the mission but neither of them wanted to do that.

Bona thought of Sister Teresa. He had to admit she was special. She was tender but she was tough. They were so different, or was it they were so alike. When they were at the high valley he thought how wonderful it would be if the three of them could be together. The afternoon was growing short as they suddenly topped a ridge and saw the town.

They pulled their horses up to a walk, "Tommy. How would you like to help me build a log house? How would you like to go back up to that valley? Build a log cabin and raise some cattle and horses?"

"I would love it. Anything, I'll do anything." The excitement was boiling in him. Tommy always showed his emotions. When he was depressed you could tell and when he was happy you could tell. Bona thought how bad a poker player he would be but what fun he was to be around.

The next morning, the sun was bright, with the start of a new adventure for Bona and Tommy. Driving a team of strong black geldings he and Tommy started out early. The wagon was loaded with everything they would need. Their saddle horses tied on behind. Tommy had a sack of rock candy and Bona had visions of something grand.

The rambling adobe buildings set inside the adobe walls looked majestic, almost royal. St. Anthony's mission had come to mean so many things to Bona. As he pulled the team to a halt at the gate, both of their eyes were on the door of the old Spanish mission, it was time.

The door opened and she appeared on the steps. She was lovely. A lump formed in Bona's throat. Never had he felt the way he did at this moment. He remembered the first time they met. The times she was a pain in the butt and the many times she was a special comfort. He was sure he had special feelings for this woman and he felt sure she returned the feelings. She was dressed as he had seen her that first night.

She was dressed in flowing black, the habit of her order. She didn't move from the top step, it was as if she were nailed in place. Tears ran down her face, her fists clenched tight at her sides. Tommy was the only one who could speak.

"Sister Teresa, We're going to build a home in the valley." Tommy had never seen her in her habit. He didn't understand what it meant. Bona understood. He understood all too well. He turned the team away from the gate. He didn't look back, he couldn't.

"You going to just drive away?" Tommy spat the question at Bona. She was still standing on the top step. "Bona, stop and go back. Please!" He never dreamed this would happen, he reached for Bona's arm but his hand was shrugged off. She watched them disappear from view, tears blinding her vision. Her prayers would always be with them even if she couldn't be. She could let them go but she could never forget them.

Bona wanted to talk, to explain to Tommy why it was just the two of them but he couldn't. He felt as if the world was coming apart. He wanted to yell at Tommy to shut up, to eat his candy and leave him alone but he couldn't do that. He had wanted to get rid of this busy-body nun for weeks, now that she was gone he was miserable. He felt so defeated, he felt like he did as a boy when the Arab died in his arms. His eyes filled with tears, his lip quivered. He felt like crying but he couldn't do that either.

Chapter Twenty-two

The winds in the pines made a musical sound, somewhere in the distance a wolf lifted his head to the moon and gave a long mournful call. The fire fluttered in the light breeze. It was magnificent but lonely. Neither of them ever spoke of Sister Teresa but they both thought of her daily.

They worked side by side, Tommy doing a man's share of the work. The log home would have open beams with a loft over the kitchen and bedrooms. A big stone fireplace with flag stone around it almost filled the other end of the cabin. The logs hewn and fitted with care. Bona was a fair hand with an axe and the two of them worked the cross-cut saw. They worked from sun up to sun down. Some nights Tommy was so sore and tired he would almost fall asleep eating his supper. It was more than just a cabin, it would be a log home. A home fit for a family.

Only when they needed fresh meat would they take a break. Tommy looked forward to these hunting and fishing trips. He was getting to be a fair hand at tracking game and shooting the rifle. As for fishing, most of the time he had better luck than Bona.

The valley was prime grazing land, nestled in the mountains with Ponderosa Pine all around. They built the cabin up against a steep rock wall. There was a small spring coming out of the rocks and they directed it into the kitchen so that they always had clean fresh water. A fine southern exposure looked out and down on the valley. The pines around the cabin gave it shade and a distinctive clean, savory smell. The walls were solid logs fitted one to the other without a crack or crevice. It had tight fitted plank flooring, not the dirt floor of most cabins and real glass in the windows. Well, all but one window that glass had been broken on their trip to the valley.

Bona poured himself another cup of coffee and watched the flames of their small fire. Tommy had eaten the last piece of trout and was already sound asleep. This land had everything, it was designed perfect. The Lord had done his work well.

Bona enjoyed the days but the nights were lonely. He would dream. In his dreams as in his life he could never have the woman. She would disappear. He was angry with himself for dreaming of something he couldn't have. He worked out his frustration with the axe and saw.

What a turn his life had taken. A few months ago he lived day to day. Worried only about himself and Buck. Now he was building a cabin, he hadn't worked so hard in years. He wasn't happy and he hurt most of the time. He was patient when it was difficult to be patient, he was agreeable when he felt disagreeable. He tried to be cheerful when he wasn't and he talked when he wanted to be silent. Something kept him going when stopping would have been so easy. He was doing his very best to understand this complex change his life was taking.

The fire became glowing coals, giving of a type of hypnotic drowsiness. The stars were like bright fireflies over the valley. He could smell the coolness of the night air. He stretched his stiff muscles, pulled off his boots and crawled into his bedroll. He felt an illusion that he was drifting off into space.

Awakening in the gray morning light, Bona heard the patter of rain on the aspen leaves. It wasn't even a sprinkle, just a drop every second or so. The rain drops were so large they sounded like hail stones or rocks hitting the leaves. The number increased. Soon it would be pouring, a real gully washer was building up.

"Tommy. Better get your buns to the cabin." Tommy jumped up and grabbing his bedroll he followed Bona into the half built cabin. Under the loft they found shelter from the rain. There was even some dry wood and ends of logs to build a fire.

"Going to try out the fireplace." It was at the other end of the cabin and rain was falling in between the loft and the fireplace. He got the fire started and the burning wood held a smell gathered by the trees for many years. The pine pitch would cause the flame to flare up, burning a bright reddish-yellow.

"I may get a little wet cooking breakfast but it will be worth it."

"What you fixing?"

"Hot cakes with venison steak, going to make some biscuits and gravy too." A young buck hung from a cross beam. Bona cut man sized steaks for both of them. The mountain air and hard work gave Tommy an appetite like a young bear just out of hibernation.

They enjoyed their meal. This figured to be an easy day. A day to lean back and rest. A day to sharpen their tools. A sharp cutting edge made the work easier. They had a Hudson Bay axe, a double-bit crown axe and several Connecticut wedges. There was a trick to using a wet-stone but Bona was a good teacher and Tommy learned quickly. It was a lazy day. A day their thoughts drifted. Tommy's thoughts drifted from the high valley to the old Spanish mission.

"Bona. Can we ride back to the mission and just ask her to join us?" He worked on an axe as he spoke. He didn't lift his eyes from the axe, he didn't want to see the expression on Bona's face.

"No."

"But Bona...."

"After the cabin is finished, we get a few head of breeding stock, we'll give her another chance. We won't beg or use any pressure. Just let her know what we have and that she is welcome to join us." He reached for the coffee pot and a cheroot.

"How can she refuse?" Tommy's eyes twinkled with joy. The sky was still dark and cloudy, it was still raining but to Tommy the day had become much brighter.

In the days that followed, Bona cut logs and Tommy used the team to drag them to the cabin site. He got along fine with the team and enjoyed snaking the logs. They made a corral out of lodge pole pine, lashing them together with rawhide. It was hard work but it was work that had to be done, so they did it.

The cabin was a regular fort. Bona knew the benefit of having a solid place to fight from. He knew the peacefulness of the valley could change quickly. It could become a battle ground. He had seen a body staked out for the ants, a fire built on a man's stomach. A man or woman had to be strong just to battle Mother Nature in this country. All the folks that talked about the romantic life in the West, lived east of the Mississippi River. They had soft chairs, cast iron stoves, feather tick beds and no Indians to fight. Indians were fighting people. Fighting was their greatest sport. Before the white man invaded their land they fought each other. Now they joined together to fight the white eyes.

Life of the Indian was much different from that of the white man. So different that most whites didn't understand their values. When the men were not out on a hunt or fighting, they sat around the village and smoked. They were not ashamed of their idleness while the women worked. It was their job to hunt and to protect the village, not to do the work of the women. One of the problems of whites moving onto the land was the protection of these villages. The Indian felt the very presence of the white man was a threat to their way of life. For that very reason, the log house may have to serve as a fort.

It was not just the Indian that could be a threat. There were bands of renegades and outlaws, men from the Civil War looking to steal anything of value and kill those that owned it.

Bona hoped that he could live in peace with the Indian, but he knew the Indian varied as much in personality, character and bravery as did the white man. There were Indians who were nothing more than savages just as there were white men who were like the ones that killed Father Francis and Sister Esther. He wanted to be prepared, prepared to defend his home against anyone that might attack.

The door and windows of the cabin were sawed in after the walls were up. He had built shutters to close in case of attack. The door was constructed with a wooden latch on the inside. It could be opened from the outside by a rawhide rope that ran through a hole. At night the latch string was pulled in so the door could not be opened from the outside. During the day it was left hanging out. The shutters had slots cut for shooting.

A rough table, chairs and cupboard were their only furniture. Their beds were bunks made with log pole pine and deer skin. The deer skin was attached to the poles with rawhide. They put their bed rolls on the deer skin. Bona had built a large bed in his bedroom but he did not have a feather tick so he slept on the smaller bunk of deer skin.

Their days seemed to drift together. Dawn to dusk was filled with work. Soon they had done all that needed to be done. The cabin was completed as was the log barn and corral.

They were both very proud of what they had built. Life could be like the nighttime sky. It could be dark and gloomy or it could glitter with a million stars. Right now as they looked at what they had accomplished their sky was bright with pride and a commitment to the future.

Chapter Twenty-three

A lanky young puncher tossed the end of his rope over the branch of a spreading willow tree. Grabbing the dangling end, he formed a hangman's knot. It was the code of the West to hang a horse thief. The puncher put the noose over his head and pulled it tight.

The rope cut at his windpipe, he wanted to make one last appeal but knew it was useless. Helplessly he waited. They had caught him with the horse and soon he would be swinging lifelessly from the branch above his head.

"Too bad your string's run out." The cattleman said, "An old mossy-horn like you should have better sense."

"I didn't steal your horse." The cowhand tied the end of the rope to the trunk of the willow.

"Ya got anything more to say?"

A wave of fear swept over the man. He had seen many a man hung, legs threshing, the life choked from their body or their neck broke if the hangman knot was done right. It was inconceivable that it could happen to him.

The thud of horses at a gallop brought every head around. They froze, granite-faced as the buckskin slid to a stop. Bona's

Colt covered the hangman as his surveyed the prisoner, rope, and punchers.

"You lawman, judge and jury?"

"Just stringing up a horse thief," retorted one of the cowhands, his tone belligerent.

"Better take him to the law," Bona sat and spoke soft and easy but they could not miss the stubborn edge to his words.

"Can't spare the time," the apparent leader of the bunch replied with disgust. His sun faded mustache under a thin beak of a nose gave him a hawk like appearance.

"He may deserve to hang but that is for a jury to say. Take the rope loose before his horse bolts, he hangs and my Colt goes off."

"Be damned if I will!"

"You think the pleasure of hanging this old man is worth your life?"

"You try to stop us and you're the dead man"

"The big question you must answer is if you're willing to bet your life I won't kill you before your punchers get me or that rifle up behind me won't knock you off your cowpony?"

For the first time they noticed Tommy with his rifle covering them on a knoll fifty yards away. At first glance they saw only the rifle not the fact that it was a boy holding it.

Photo by Angee

No one made a move. Slowly they all turned to the man Bona had threatened. He nodded reluctantly. A puncher untied the rope from the tree. Their eyes burned with hate for Bona. They felt the only man lower than a horse thief was a man who protected one.

"B'Gawd! You've put your damn nose into something that is none of your business." The man raged as one of the punchers jerked the rope from the limb as the old-timer awkwardly slid off the horse. He lifted the rope from the man's neck and coiled it up. The man who had been so near death limped over behind Buck. He was a little over weigh, with silver-gray hair. A clean shaven face, and thick eyebrows that almost touched above his nose. He didn't understand this strange turn of events but he was thankful.

"Take your horse. You're not out anything and no one has to die here today." Slowly they turned their mounts. Bona did not want to talk, one of them could do something stupid and several would surely die. Bona watched as they rode away, leading the rider less horse.

"Did you really long-rope that horse?" Bona continued to watch the riders.

"He just wandered into my camp but I was scared I was going to hang for it."

"Where's your things?" Bona still watched the departing riders.

"Over yonder," he pointed to a clump of bushes as Tommy rode up. He limped toward his camp.

"My leg's stiffer'n a fence post," he explained apologetically. "I was out here holding the horse when they rode up, they didn't give me a chance to show them Maud."

Behind some bushes was all he had in the world. An old McClellan saddle, his bedroll, a few supplies and a mule. There seemed to be something special about this man. Bona had noticed it first when he sat on the horse with the noose around his neck. Just a slap of the horse's rump away from death yet he showed no hate for the men who were doing what they thought was right.

"Best ride with us a ways. This is Tommy. Tommy Burns and I'm Bona King."

"Name's Red Murphy but all the red has turned to silver." He was busy packing his few things. He lifted the McClellan which was a cross between a western saddle and an English with a deep comfortable seat to the back of his mule. "This is Maud best mule and friend a man could have." She was a large mule, almost as big as Buck. Bona knew the advantages of a mule over a horse, he had seen it in the war. They adopted to weather easier, were less likely to overeat or overdrink and could handle cheaper, coarser foods. They had strong hooves, lots of stamina and were sure footed.

From a saddlebag Red pulled an old U.S. Army field glass. He handed it to Bona to check the riders. They seemed to have lost their desire for a hanging. He watched as they crossed a stream and tuned into a canyon with ferns and trees growing from the rock walls. A moment later they disappeared from view. He handed the glass back to Red.

"They seem to be on their way home." The sun was sinking in the west and in another hour it would be below the ridgeline. Bona wanted to travel and put as much distance between them and the punchers as was possible. He took the lead, being careful to scan every hillside for signs of trouble. The rays of the sun reflected off a few large thunderheads rolling in from the west. They were riding in a sandy drainage ditch only a dozen feet wide. It was still very warm in the bottom of the ravine. It was dusk and growing darker by the minute. He watched Buck's ears as Buck would see or smell anyone approaching long before he would. Bucks ears would tell him if they were riding into trouble.

As darkness settled in, they found an excellent camp site. A spring plunging out of the mountainside formed a pool the size of a pool table. It was over knee deep in the middle, good clear water. Good meadow grass surrounded the pool and dead coals in a circle of rocks showed the spot had been used by others. Wood for a fire was all around.

"Where you gents headed?" Red asked as he kindled a small fire.

"Looking for some stock. Got a nice valley back a ways." Bona put the coffee pot on to boil. Tommy got the jerked venison and biscuits out.

"What you traipsing around these mountains for?" Tommy came right to the point.

"This and that. Mostly just to see what's on the other side of the hill." He had a twinkle of Irish merriment in his ice blue eyes. This appealed to both Bona and Tommy.

Chapter Twenty-four

"There is no such thing as pure innocence, even tiny babies carry within them the sins of centuries of wrong doing and thinking." Two crimson marks were etched into the sides of the priest's nose from the round, steel framed spectacles he wore. With these in his hand, he turned from his walnut secretary where he sat.

"You can't be perfect, no one can be perfect. Your biggest battle is in your mind." Father Joseph frowned, his pale near sighted eyes always looked as if he was peering into the distance.

Sister Teresa, her face ashen against the black and white starched wimple and bib. Her heavy skirt swishing the floor as she paced. The room, with its thick whitewashed adobe walls carved joints and open beams gave off an environment where the Lord could do battle with any evil omens or ancient shadows that may exist.

"Satan seems to be destroying your thinking," the priest put on his glasses as if to better see her problem.

"I pray and the words seem wrong."

"Temptations are inevitable. As certain as the sun rises in the east, temptations will daily enter our thoughts." The padre took up his pipe and began to fill the bowl from the humidor on his desk.

"Father, I just don't understand what the Lord wants of me."

"You are doing excellent work with the children. Speaking of the children, do you remember my lecture to them yesterday? I told them to eliminate the things that got in their way, to be original in their solutions to the tasks they faced. Not to be afraid, to work to their full potential. To do everything you were created to do you have to take chances. I told them that their dreams and visions could be an asset or a source of failure. God helps those who help themselves. What is true for the children is also true for us. Like the children you too must use creative problem solving." The old padre spoke first in English but finished his words in Spanish.

She nodded her head in agreement and with her eyes glistening with tears, Sister Teresa went to the altar and knelt before the crucifix. With rosary beads dangling from fingers tense with confusion and fear, she prayed. She made her confession expressing penitence in the light of the tapers. If only she could clear up the eternal pain in her heart.

Somberly considering the twist of destiny that caused her pain. She remembered Bona and Tommy. The intensity of her memory shocked her. She had been sure that once back at the mission she would not think of them as being so important in her life.

"Please Lord. Show me how to carry this cross you have asked me to bear. Give me the strength and courage to banish all sadness and to receive your bountiful blessings. Let me accept wholeheartedly the correct alternatives. Let me be patient for what I will become is known only by you."

Chapter Twenty-five

The wild herd of mustangs had grown strong of limb and restless of spirit. They had never known human restraints or comforts. They had never had the sweetness of grain or the confines of a corral. They had survived driving storms, learned to find water and food where there appeared to be none. They were wild and free roving the mountains. Arab blood showed in the strength and beauty of their high held heads.

Bona watched the herd with Red's field glass. He studied the herd going from one horse to the next. He settled on the stallion who was always behind his herd, driving the mares and foals. He was glassy black with one hind sock and a small blaze. This same coloring showed in many of the foals.

"Cunning devil, aren't you?" The stallion turned to look in Bona's direction. They were well hid and down wind, several hundred yards away. Yet the stallion acted as if he knew they were there.

"That's a beautiful stallion, can we get him?" They watched the black drive his herd up a narrow canyon lined with trees and brush. This opened into a large valley where the herd grazed. They had used this same trail many times, it would be an ideal spot for a horse trap.

"He's worth more right where he is." Bona still held the glass to his eye.

"Bona's right. Best leave him run wild."

"We want a few two year olds, a few good mares with foals at their said and another in their belly." Bona watched as the herd went out of sight.

They rode to the canyon and shook out their loops. They had to snake deadfall logs into spaces between the trees. They would have to cut some lodge pole to fill in where there weren't enough deadfalls. Using the forks of the trees and lashing the poles in place, they fashioned a crude but sturdy corral. Brush and tumbleweeds were used to help conceal their work. It was not hard work and the finished just before sundown.

They didn't want to start a fire, the smell would linger in the canyon and warn the stallion. So they ate jerky and drank from their canteens. Tommy had never been on a horse hunt and he had a million questions. Bona and Red took turns being as patient as was possible. His questions were helpful as they allowed Bona and Red to cover all the possible problems that could arise. They were all tired and during one of Red's long drawn-out answers to a simple yes or no question, Tommy fell asleep.

The night was short, Bona rolled them out of their sacks before sun up. After some jerky and a drink of warm water, they used tumbleweeds to sweep out their tracks. They could open either end of their trap depending of the direction of the wind. The slight breeze was from the west so they opened the west end.

Red took Maud and worked his way around behind where they hoped the wild herd bedded down for the night. Tommy and Bona took their horses to the east side and tied them in a clump of brush out of sight. Now the wait began. Morning was just starting to paint a sunrise in the east. The faint color slowly becoming a big red ball that turned into sparkling daylight.

Everything was in their favor. The wind would be at the back of the herd and the sun would be in their eyes. Bona felt sure the stallion would drive them through the canyon into their trap.

Bona had great respect for these horses. Horses that run free but have ancestors that have been domesticated are not truly "wild" horses; they are feral horses. These horses escaped from the Spanish and formed feral herds. Best known as the mustang most everyone considered them wild. They survived hard times. Their leader was cunning and had avoided capture. Their one desire was to remain free but once they learned the human hand would not harm them they became good stock.

Slowly Red moved into view of the herd. When he was still more than a mile away the black warned the herd. With head and tail aloft, mane and tail black streamers in the wind, he gave a neigh and moved his band away from the approaching danger. His shrill neigh and sharp flashing teeth drove the herd. His noble head erect, nostrils flaring he leaped into a trot behind the herd. The stallion had no reason to look for a trap where they ran only yesterday.

Into the narrow canyon they raced, down the trail and into the waiting trap. The stallion recovered too late to save his herd. Tommy and Bona had a lodge pole in place to close the trap behind the herd. When they came to the fence they veered off, milling in dust and confusion. Tossing his head with rage the black wheeled. He did his best to force the mares through the fence. When this failed he lifted his voice and called to them to follow as he leaped the fence to freedom. Most of the herd did not have his power and grace. A couple of the two year olds jumped the fence but the mares and foals were trapped by the logs and trees.

Bona and Tommy watched as the band of horses roamed the trap looking for an opening to escape. When none could be found, they gradually settled down.

"Oh look!" Tommy pointed to a foal down with one front leg bent under him. The little fella looked just like his daddy who had leaped to freedom.

"Broken wheel," Bona said and Red nodded in agreement from the back of Maud. Bona crossed the fence and carefully worked his way to the side of the injured foal. One good look confirmed his assumption, the leg was broken. The little guy had to be put out of his misery. Bona couldn't do it in the corral, a shot would send the herd through the fence or injure others.

The little colt didn't want Bona to touch him. He threshed about until he got to his feet. Hobbling unsteadily on three legs he moved away from Bona. Red's rope sang out and settled around his neck. With the herd at the other end of the corral they worked him through the fence.

One by one they tied his feet together. They had to be careful not to get hit by the sharp hooves. Being as gentle as possible they rolled him onto a tarp from Red's bedroll. Red drug him slowly back down the narrow canyon. After ten or fifteen minutes they heard the distant sound of Red's old Colt Dragoon.

"Wasn't there anything we could do?"

"Just put him out of his misery as quick as possible." Bona took a cheroot from his pocket. He had wanted a smoke all morning.

"Why did you tie up his feet?"

"You should always beware of a wounded animal, they can be very dangerous."

When Red returned, Bona had a fire going and coffee on. Tommy, stood with a foot up on the corral rail, watching the horses paw and mill about. A cloud of yellow dust hung in the air. After they had eaten, they began the task of sorting out the horses they wanted to keep. Red held the gate at the east end letting the culls out. After an hour they had six mares with foals and a couple nice two/three year olds remaining in the corral.

"We'll let them stand tonight without any food or water," Bona checked the gate on the west end of the small corral.

"Why?" Tommy asked following Bona.

"Because we want them to get to depend on us," Bona walked back to the camp fire and poured himself a cup of coffee. "It's still a while before dark, why don't you guys see if you can catch a mess of fish for supper? I noticed a nice trout stream only a mile or so up the trail, I'll keep an eye on our catch."

Only a faint suggestion of dawn was showing in the east when they finished their hurried breakfast. "Better take something with you. We won't be stopping to eat." Bona picked up some left over bacon and put it in his shirt pocket.

Squatting by the fire, Red nodded his head in agreement. "Little of that cold trout will taste good about mid-day. Wrap me a piece or two." He tossed Tommy his extra bandanna from his saddle bag.

"Red you and Maud take the point, Tommy and I will push them along as slow as possible. Take the same trail we came down. They will smell water and should go right to it."

"Better keep an eye out for the black devil, he may try to steal his mares back." Red got to his feet and went to get his mule. He wanted to get a hundred feet head start as they could come out of the gate like a bat-out-of-Hell.

As the gate was swung open, an old mustang mare took the lead. She pricked her ears and whinnied but she heard no answering whinny. She fell into an easy lope behind Red on Maud. It was what Bona hope and expected to happen. After the horses drank their fill at the stream they settled into a nice trot. These mustangs could trot like this all day and still have a spurt of speed if they needed it.

A cloud of dust rolled up that could be seen for miles. Bona hoped there weren't any unfriendly Indians in the area to spot it. Once they got a mile or two higher up in the mountain the trees would help block the sign. A few times a mare attempted to break away from the bunch but Bona or Tommy quickly cut her off. The trail was narrow which also helped to keep them bunched. They were in a habit of following and not accustomed to making decisions so it was only natural for them to follow Maud.

All day the trail twisted higher and higher into the heart of the mountain. They passed the spot where Red almost stretched the hangman's rope, climbing higher into their own valley. Bona sat and watched the band of mares fan out in the rich grazing. There was something unique about having his own land and horses that gave him a rare feeling of importance. The lone wolf drifter had found something better than filling an inside straight.

Tommy and Red put the poles in place to close the valley off. As they rode up beside Bona, still staring at the now grazing mustangs, Red broke the magic spell.

"Got yourself a mighty pretty place."

"This valley just naturally seems to latch onto me."

"Let's get some grub, my belly is pushing against by backbone." Red put his heels to Maud and started for the cabin.

"You rode up front, we ate all the dust," Tommy turned his horse to follow.

"If you don't hurry you'll eat my dust again." It was a challenge Tommy couldn't resist. He put his horse into a gallop, leaning over its neck like a jockey. As they raced, Bona watched with a smile growing on his face.

Chapter Twenty-Six

A fat Mexican in a dirty white shirt stood behind the bar. Two leather chapped cowboys stood nearby, drinking tequila. There were several round tables and at one of them sat two men. The new sawdust on the floor helped to cut the stale smoke and alcohol smell.

All eyes turned to Bona as he entered. Everything from the roll of a man's hat to his spurs told something about him. None of the eyes missed the tied-down Colt on his left hip. Nor did they miss the fact that when he went to the corner of the bar to order a drink, his left hand hung at his side near the butt of his Colt.

"You have come far, senor?"

"Far enough, I am dry and hungry."

"If you will have a seat, my wife will bring food. What would you like to drink?" The barkeep turned toward the kitchen, holding up one finger as a signal.

"A beer." Bona dropped wearily into a chair at the nearest table. He removed his hat and combed his hair with his fingers. He rubbed the stubble on his chin and thought how great a hot bath and shave would feel.

The meal was a plate of beans, beef and tortillas. It was hot and tasty. There was also a wedge of apple pie. When the bartender came to see if he needed anything else, Bona asked if he knew of anyone with stock cows for sale. He nodded toward the table where two men were sharing a bottle.

Bona pushed back his chair and got up. "Excuse me," he said as he stepped up to their table. "Understand you may some stock cows for sale."

The old man was rail thin with hard brown eyes and snow white hair. The last two years around Salida had been dry. Even the Current River was as low as any could remember. The old rancher looked up into Bona's blue gray eyes as he reached for the bottle.

"Could have a small bunch of old mossy horned range cows for sale." Bona could see he was a fighting man but the one thing a rancher couldn't fight was the lack of water. He had too many cows for these conditions.

"I will be leaving at daylight, about a day's ride east." He poured three fingers in his glass and nodded toward the bottle.

"No thanks," Bona wasn't much of a drinking man. Being on the drift most of his life he couldn't afford to be under the influence of cheap booze. Alcohol dissolves almost anything, including a man's judgement. Bona had seen it cause men to do things they later regretted. Staying alive had always been one of his top priorities.

"Meet you here for breakfast?" The old rancher nodded his head and lifted his glass in a half salute.

As Bona turned to place his empty beer mug on the bar he found the barkeep waiting.

"Would Senor like a room?"

"Yes, and a hot bath would be nice." He reached in his pocket and came out with several coins. He placed a five dollar gold piece on the bar and got a silver dollar in change.

"I will have your horse taken care of too senor." He turned and snapped his fingers at a small wiry boy. He placed a key on the bar and pointed toward an open stairway.

Bona went outside followed by the boy. He removed his saddlebags and bedroll, pulled his rifle and spoke to the boy in Spanish.

"Give him some grain and all he wants to drink, he's cooled down enough so it won't hurt him." Bona flipped the boy a silver dollar and his eyes got as big as horse biscuits.

"Si, senor."

When Bona got to his room he found hot water and a clean towel waiting. The wooden tub was too small for his to sit down but standing in the hot water he washed off the trail dust and shaved. With a chair under the doorknob and his Colt within easy reach he crawled into bed. In seconds he was asleep.

As Bona ate his steak and eggs a rooster crowed out back as if expressing his pleasure in the part he played in Bona's breakfast. The old rancher was having a large breakfast. Bona wondered how the man stayed so thin the amount of grub he put away.

"So, you got a spread around here?"

"A long day's ride west of here. Just built a cabin and have a few mustang mares with foals and want some stock cows."

"You got a family?" He poured both cups full of hot steaming coffee as he asked.

"No. Couple friends. A ten year old boy and an old codger." Bona wondered how funny that must sound.

"Man needs a woman. I had the best. Lost her a year ago this winter."

"Oh, sorry to hear that." Bona didn't know just what to say, he wasn't much good at making small talk about death.

"Nothing in this man's world compares to the love of a good woman." He leaned back in his chair to roll a smoke.

"To love a person is to do what's best for them and sometimes that's riding away." Bona didn't know why he said that to a complete stranger. Maybe it was in the back of his mind and just had to get out. Whatever the reason it caused the old rancher to stop rolling his cigarette and look at Bona. He was thinking about what Bona had said. It wasn't something the average cowhand would come up with. He wanted to ask him to explain but thought better of it.

All the valley needed to make it as pretty as Bona's high mountain meadow was water. Even the clumps of aspen and dwarf willows looked to be in need of a drink. The grass was brown. This valley needed a heavy rain, a soaking two day rain. The chance of that was slim as they were in the dry season. A twenty feet dry rocky bed showed where a stream normally ran. What a huge difference water or the lack of water could make. Under normal conditions this valley could feed hundreds of wildlife. The valley seemed empty.

When Bona sighted the ranch building he knew just how big a spread this was. The bunk house looked to be fifty feet long, enough space to sleep twenty men. The barns and out buildings were impressive but it was the main house that took your eye. Big and sprawling it had lots of large glass windows. A porch with a rail ran all along the front side. Bona could see three big stone chimneys indicating as many fireplaces.

A horse whinnied and a dog barked from the doorway to what Bona thought was the blacksmith shop. Several large corrals stood empty but one small lot by the horse barn held a half dozen saddle horses. A large wooden windmill, the fan turning in the wind was not pumping water into the round wooden tank.

A girl followed the dog out of the door and waved a greeting. Dressed in a long riding skirt, with a blue plaid blouse she looked as if she had just stepped out of the Sears Roebuck catalogue.

"Hi dad, you have a good trip?" She was lovely, dark eyed with dark hair.

"Yes, fine." He swung down and gave her a kiss on the forehead. "Jayne, this is Bona King, he is interested in buying a few head of stock cows." She turned and held her hand out to him. "Bona, this is my daughter, Jayne."

They shock hands, Bona noticed the firmness of her grip and her searching eyes. She looked him over like a horse trader examining a new deal. She didn't even make an attempt to hide what she was doing. She was mighty pretty but she made him feel a little uncomfortable. Her dog, a wolf type, stood at her side. He followed Bona's every move, ready to spring into action if necessary. Bona took Buck to the tank and let him have a little water. He didn't want him to drink too much, too soon. Jayne took her father's horse and did likewise.

"You have a ranch near here?"

"Have a cabin and a few horses in a nice high valley, three days west of here." Bona pulled Buck away from the tank.

"Find an empty stall in the barn and help yourself to hay and grain." Bona found what he was looking for, stripped Buck and rubbed him down before giving him hay and grain. The girl took care of her dad's horse. She was petite, slim and lovely but she handled the big Texas saddle without any trouble. She appeared to know her way around horses.

Bona couldn't remember when he had been in a more elegant home. Seated at a large round table in the dining room with Jayne and her father. Jayne had changed and was wearing a dark green dress that showed off her fine figure. She had a touch of artificial color on her cheeks and lips. She looked to be a little younger than Bona but it was difficult to tell.

"How much grass do you have?"

"About a thousand acres I would guess. It's a high valley with bluffs of sheer rock on three sides. We have built a rail fence across the open east end." Bona ate daintily, not because he wasn't hungry or the food tasty but because of the setting.

The fine crystal, cloth napkins and engraved silverware was far more than he was accustomed to.

"So you have good grazing and plenty of water?"

"Yes sir."

"How many cows do you want?"

"As many as you will sell me for three hundred dollars."

The old rancher thought for a moment before answering. "I will let you have fifty head. All with a calf at their side and one in their belly. That's three for the price of one."

"That's very generous of you." Bona was doing the math in his head.

"I will on one condition," the old rancher added.

"What's the one condition?"

"That you also take five hundred head of mine and graze them for a year." He pushed back his chair and got a box of cigars from the hitch. He offered one to Bona.

"Don't see any reason we couldn't do that, we got plenty of grazing and water." Bona took a cigar and accepted a light from his host.

"Now that the business is settled and the men have their cigar, may a lady enter the conversation?" After a short pause and with a touch of laughter she added.

"A lady can't mix in business or enjoy a good cigar after dinner."

"Oh, I'm sorry. Did you want a cigar?" As her father spoke he picked up the box of cigars and extended his arm toward his daughter.

"No thank you. I learned at that fancy school you sent me to that it was not proper."

"Okay, what about the business? What did you want to add there?" His voice had a sarcastic bite to it.

"What about hay? You're going to need a great deal of hay for the winter." It was a good question, one they had not talked about.

"The men that make the drive will have to stay and cut and stack some hay. A week of making hay should do it." He puffed his cigar, sending up a cloud of smoke around his head. He appeared to be happy with the deal.

"I didn't see any hands when we rode in." Bona too was enjoying the good cigar.

"All my hands are up in the north country, moving cows from one small valley to the next. It's the only grass we have. We have to stay right with them, if they ever got scattered in that country it would take a hundred men a year to round them up. That is why your valley sounds so appealing to me."

"We sold all we could to the army at Fort Logan but we have to have stock for when the grass down here does come back." Jayne was more than just a pretty daughter, she was like a partner with her father.

"You take your pick of the bunks, Shorty is the only man we have here. In the morning we will ride up and sort out your cows. We can add a brand to them so we know the difference. You got a brand?"

"Nothing registered. Planned to register a cross brand."

"Shorty is good with iron, he will make us a couple cross branding irons." He pushed back his chair and got to his feet. He excused himself, leaving the two young people at the table.

Jayne smiled, saying nothing. Bona was feeling rather uncomfortable. Just the presence of this lovely young lady was enough to make his pulse quicken. He was embarrassed but hoped it didn't show. He was also worried that what he was thinking showed in his face.

"You attended a school back East?" He hoped the question was enough for her to take control of the conversation.

"Father sent me to Chicago. I stayed with my mother's brother and his wife. This was after my mother passed away." Her eyes widened, she took a deep breath and continued. "And you, what and who is Bona King?"

"After the war I just kind of drifted this way. My partners are a ten year old orphan boy and a grandfather type who was almost hanged as a horse thief."

"Sounds like an interesting crew. Would you care for a glass of brandy?"

"That would be fine if you are having some."

She poured them each some brandy in large round snifters. Bona was afraid he would crush his glass as it so thin. He watched her to see how to hold it. She took a sip, so Bona did likewise.

"Let's go out on the porch, I so enjoy the view from there." Without waiting for him to answer, she led the way. The sky was filled with thousands of pin points of light. The moon, just a slice, was bright in the clear sky.

From out of the darkness, almost like a ghost, her dog joined them and positioned himself between them.

"Tell me how you came about having an orphan boy and a grandfather type for your partners." She took a sip of her brandy, the moonlight seemed to add to her beauty.

"Well, Tommy's mother died and he was in a bad situation. Didn't have any family so I let him tag along with me. We came upon Red about to be hung for stealing a horse and I talked them into not being judge and jury as well as hangmen. After hearing his story I don't think he would steal anything. He seems to be well educated but has not shared his life story with us yet." Bona took a sip of the brandy hoping his short version was enough to satisfy her.

"They back at your spread?"

"Yes, they are holding down the fort while I try to get some stock cows. Your father has made me a generous offer."

"Well, to be honest, he doesn't have many options. We have no grass, very little hay and we need these cows when we do get grass."

Chapter Twenty-seven

"So this nun just ups and waves good-bye without an aye, yes, or no?" Red was working on a rocking chair. Tommy was making a three legged stool.

Photo by Brent

"She didn't even wave goodbye," he put down the stool and went to sit on the edge of the porch. He watched the foals run and play. They were getting tamer every day. He could get several to them to come up and eat out of his hand. Red had helped him put rope halters on them. One foal, a little horse colt he named Black Rhythm was even getting to be broke to lead.

"Wanted Bona to go back but he wouldn't. She just stood on the mission steps, dressed in her black church clothes watching us ride away."

"Those foals should have some oats when we take them off their mother's milk." Red spoke soft, in a mumble like he was thinking out loud. About half the time Tommy had to guess at what he was saying. He did repeat himself a lot which helped Tommy get the message.

"You think we can do anything?"

"About what, Tommy?"

"About Bona and Sister Teresa, I really miss her and I think Bona does too."

"The fact is, no one can shape a life according to their way of thinking it should be. Nor should he try. A woman has to do things her way and a man has to face his problems his way. You're only asking for trouble if you mix in."

"So we just sit and do nothing?"

"Didn't say that. I only said you're asking for trouble." He worked on the walnut chair like a man enjoying his creation.

"What do you mean?"

"We could kind of give things a push and see where they end up."

"How?"

"Don't rightly know. We'll have to do some thinking. See if we can't come up with an idea." Red got up and went into the cabin, returning with a book. He handed it to Tommy, a worn copy of Ride Proud, a book about the Sioux Indians by a man who had never been west of the Mississippi River.

"Being you run out of work for the time being, read me some of this."

Tommy read in spurts, when he came to a word he didn't recognize or a sentence he couldn't make out, he would ask Red. Sometimes he would read a whole sentence to himself, figure it out, and then read it again out loud. He followed the line of print with his finger. Once he worked it out in his mind, made sense of what was written, he would read it to Red with confidence and delight.

"Is this true? Do you think Indians are dirty savages, lacking human control?" Tommy looked up from the book, doubt showing on his face.

"Indians are fighting people. Fighting is a sport to them, it is their way of life. Before the white man came and gave the Indian liquor, ruined his hunting and drove him onto poor land and into poverty, the Indian was cleaner, more honest and more respectful then the white men that were coming west. He was strong, proud and had few problems." Red put a match to his pipe, puffed it to fire and continued.

"That's not to say the Indian was not fierce and that he couldn't be cruel to an enemy. It's good to read, just remember, just because it's in print, doesn't make it true."

Tommy nodded his head and went back to reading. He wished he could read as well as Red or Bona. Sister Teresa, she could read a story and you got the feeling you were right there, living the story word by word. Thinking about Sister Teresa, Tommy stopped reading and stared off into space.

"Penny for your thoughts," Red said. He had to repeat it before Tommy snapped back to the here and now.

"Just thinking about Sister Teresa," his head dropped and so did his voice as he spoke.

You kind of miss this Sister person, don't you?"

"Yes, she is special and I thought I was special to her too." Again his voice dropped and his shoulders slumped.

"Don't do any good feeling sorry for yourself. Life isn't all sweet and nice. It can be cruel and sour as Hell." Red puffed on his pipe and worked on the chair as he talked.

"I know, I have seen how cruel life can be, I just thought Sister Teresa was different, I thought my luck had changed." He turned to look at Red for an answer.

"If you look around and count your blessings you will see that it has changed. If you spend your time counting your blessing it may change even more."

Tommy knew Red was right. He was in a better place than he had ever hoped to be. It would be perfect if Sister Teresa were here too.

"You get on down there and work with the foals." Red took his pipe out of his mouth and looked at the stem as if it had taken a bite out of his tongue. "In a spell, I will come down and we'll see if we can't catch a mess of fish for supper." Tommy put the book away and took off on a run. He didn't know if he liked playing with the foals or fishing best.

Tommy had trouble working with some of the foals as Black Rhythm would come up and nuzzle him to get his attention.

The little black horse colt was jealous, he wanted Tommy to concentrate on him. Tommy could put his arm around the colt's neck and lean his other arm over Rhythm's back putting a little weight on his shoulders. Tommy could pick up the colt's feet and was almost to the point where Rhythm would let him put them back down.

"That one has decided you belong to him." Red had been standing and watching. "You ready to go see if the trout are biting?"

"Sure, bet I catch the first fish." As Tommy and Red walked toward the stream, Rhythm followed. He was a good hundred yards from his mother when she called to him. Tommy turned and waved his arm at the colt, "Go on get back to your supper." Rhythm shook his head, turned and trotted back to the herd.

Tommy, chirpy as a cock sparrow, flapped his lip about everything and anything. Red would grunt occasionally, more interested in eating the trout than in hearing what Tommy was saying. To most adults, Tommy would be a constant irritant but Red was patient. Red was a difficult man to judge. His clothes were old and worn, yet his boots were handmade and expensive like his gold pocket watch. The lines and creases of age showed on his face but his eyes were bright always full of hope and love.

Photo by Brent

Finished with his meal, Red chewed the stem of his briar pipe and drank a second cup of coffee. "You eat any more fish and you'll spurt a dorsal fin."

"Can't help it if you're as good at cooking them as I am at catching them."

Red loaded his pipe with tobacco from a leather pouch meticulously. It was as if he received as much enjoyment from packing his pipe as he did in smoking it. He was a man that paid attention to minute details in everything he did.

"You get at the dishes, let's see if you're as good at washing plates as you are emptying them."

Chapter Twenty-eight

The herd moved up the wide pass, the pace was slow and easy. Soil gave way to rock and the well-trodden trail began to slope upward. Jayne rode beside her father, no sign of fatigue showed on her face. She was the first to spot the troopers and pointed them out to her father.

A young captain rode at the head of the column of eight. They hesitated only a moment and then kept riding toward Jayne and her father. A smile broke out on the faces of both the young captain and Jayne as the recognized each other. The captain raised an arm and the men hauled on the reins to halt their mounts.

"Miss Jayne," he tipped his hat and turned to her father, "Mr. Hedges."

"Captain Stratton, what brings you this far from Fort Logan?" The herd moved past as they stopped to talk. A mist of dust settled down on them.

"After a deserter, got word he was headed in this direction," he quickly changed the subject, "And you, you're a long way from home."

"Driving these cows to a place where there is enough grass to keep them healthy."

"Is this man you're after dangerous?" Jayne asked.

"No. In fact he is a good friend. I almost hope we don't catch up to him."

"What's this man look like?"

He's an older man, almost ready to retire."

"Why did he go A.W.O.L.?" Mr. Hedges took off his hat and wiped the sweat band.

"He is wanted by the army for murder."

"Murder?'"

"It is a long story, hope I can give you all the details soon, right now we have to ride." He tipped his hat to Jayne and returned to his men. They watched as the troopers rode off.

Bona rode up as the last of the herd passed. "What is the Calvary doing, looking for Indians?" They were getting close to his place, he hoped there wasn't a raiding party in the area.

"No, they are after an Army deserter." They rode together for a ways and told Bona what they knew. It wasn't long and they came to the east line fence to his valley.

Tommy was working with a foal and Red was putting some finishing touches to his rocking chair when the herd entered the valley. The cows were so content to be in the knee deep grass that they spread out and began to graze.

"Red! It's Bona with a herd of cattle." Tommy removed his lead rope from the little filly and ran to meet the approaching riders. Waving and calling to Bona who reached down and swung him up behind him. They rode up to Jayne.

"Jayne, this is Tommy."

Tommy was struck by her beauty, even soiled from the drive he could see how pretty she was.

"So this is the young man that is your partner?"

He also noticed her honey favored flirting. He had seen women around the saloons, his mother even, turn a man's head with their sweet talk. This pretty gal had her sights set on Bona. Sometimes he thought he knew more about women than Bona did. Bona just didn't seem to understand how the mind of a women was different from that of a man.

"Yes, he helped build the cabin and corrals. Come on, I will introduce you to Red."

The next couple of weeks were filled with making hay and preparing for winter. Bona seemed to be spending more and more of his time with Jayne and less and less with Tommy. Tommy didn't know if he liked this dark haired beauty but he did know that Bona had better be careful or she would have him roped and hog tied before he knew what happened. She was a woman who got what she wanted and didn't mess with what she had no use for. Tommy didn't think she liked him. He didn't think she would share Bona with anyone, especially a ten year old orphan boy.

Chapter Twenty-nine

Sister Teresa had brought some needed changes to the mission. Using her share of the bounty money, she improved the school. She purchased new equipment to make candles and pottery. The orphans could make enough earthen pots and vessels on their new pottery wheel to support the mission. They even shipped some of the Indian pottery east where the market for the primitive art was sizable.

The financial status of the mission was so good that it had caused a fluster in the diocese. The bishop, the head administrator of the district was there to find out how it all happened. The last time he visited the mission all they had to eat was wild onion soup and bread.

"The older students keep records and make deliveries to town. We ship to several different major cities in the east." Sister Teresa was giving him a tour, showing him the records. The bishop had never seen anything like it during his priesthood. The first order of business of the mission was religion, the obedience to their faith.

"You are somewhat of a maverick Sister Teresa but your work is very impressive. Never have I seen happier children in or out of an orphanage."

"When people feel good about themselves, everything they do it better. Wait until you see them during worship. Before they just had faith. Now they can see the fruits of their faith. Before they lived on handouts. Now, by the labor of their hands and heads."

"Your books show a large cash balance. Where is this money kept?"

"There are a hundred excellent hiding places in this old mission. The money is as safe as if it were in an eastern bank. We do have an account in the local bank also."

"What are your plans for the money?"

"When each of these orphans leave here, they will have a nest egg. The children help decide what new equipment is needed and how the money is spent.

"I wonder if the surplus should not be held at the administrative office." They both knew that once the money was in the central office it would be used for the whole diocese, there would be no graduation nest egg.

"No, the money belongs to the children not the diocese. When the money is spent, the children have a vote. They have earned this right and opportunity."

The bishop was annoyed that this Sister had the courage to question his judgement. He had to admit she made some good points but he was not accustomed to being refused a request. He had never been confronted with such lack of discipline by a nun.

"I called you a maverick, your methods have been less than customary. On the other hand it is easy to see the positive results of your labor. I sincerely hope you have not over stepped you position." He turned and walked away.

In a few minutes, the bishop returned with Father Joseph. Sister Teresa could see that Father Joseph was not happy with the situation. His near-sighted eyes peered over the top of his steel framed spectacles.

"Sister Teresa," he spoke soft, hesitant. "The bishop feels that at least a portion of the surplus money should go to the central office."

"I will get the children together, the bishop can explain to them his thoughts and they will vote on it."

She started to leave.

"Wait!" The bishop was red in the face. "I do not understand why you insist on being so difficult. Orphans do not have the right to make decisions of this nature."

"They do at St. Anthony's when it was by their labor that the money was earned. You are welcome to any money from the donation box. The children will determine how and when the money they earn is spent."

"I don't understand your position and your stubbornness will not be forgotten." He stomped off.

The next morning the bishop took the stage without another word to Sister Teresa about the money. A few days later, a new priest and two nuns returned on the stage. They shared the coach with a man that appeared to sleep most of the trip. With his wide brimmed hat covering the features of his face he heard their every word. The talk of the surplus money at the mission and how they planned to get it for the central office, caused his cruel jawline to break into a smile. It was essential he got some quick cash to escape the nightmare of his past. What could be easier than taking money from a mission?

It was not difficult finding a partner at the bar and after making their plans, they rode to the mission. People were coming and going all the time so two riders coming in did not draw any attention. It wasn't until he drew his revolver and grabbed one of the children that the alarm was sounded.

Sister Teresa came running to the aid of the child. A hard hand slapped a forceful blow to her head, knocking her against the wall. Another of the children gave a screeching shriek of pain for her but Sister Teresa said nothing.

"Leave her. There's an easier way." He grabbed a small Indian girl by her hair and put his razor sharp knife to her throat. The girl sobbed with fear.

"You beast! Leave that child alone." Sister Teresa got to her feel slowly.

"Sure. Just go with my friend, get the money and I won't cut her." He looked pleased with the fear in the faces of the child and nun.

"Alright! Just be careful and don't hurt that child." She moved to the door and the man fell in behind her.

Sister Teresa took several loose brick from the wall behind the altar. She reached in and produced a tin box. She handed it to the man and watched as he opened it. The sight of the gold coins and paper bills made the man careless. His mistake was to underestimate the nun behind him.

With a smooth motion as if she were throwing a ball she cracked him behind the ear with a brick. In one quick move she took his revolver from his now lax fingers. He started to gain his balance and she hit him again, this time with his gun. His knees dipped and he fell forward on his face, his nose smashing into the stone floor. The tin box of coins and paper bills slipped from numb fingers to spill all over the floor.

Sister Teresa cocked the revolver and headed back the way she came. The blood raced in her temples at the very thought of the knife being held to the throat of little Michele. Her head was spinning with thoughts of what she could do. She put the gun in a fold of her skirt. At the door, she was hesitant. A mistake could mean several lives. The door opened into the room. She opened it just enough so the man inside could see her. She stopped, turned and looked behind her. Speaking loud but making it sound as normal as she was able.

"I gave you the money, now stop pushing me with that gun!"

She stumbled into the room as if pushed from behind. The man holding little Michele released her and she ran to one of the older children. He stood alone, holding the knife, waiting to see his partner and the money. Instead, he saw the gun in the nun's hands come to bear on this chest.

"Drop your knife. Don't make me prove I can use this."

The problem he had was that the revolver in the hands of this nun just did not appear to be too threatening. He could throw his knife, he had done it before. She was a nun, she would hesitate and that would be all that was required for him to kill her. His hand made a quick move to throw the knife and the revolver bucked fire. The slug caught him in the breastbone, shattering bone and driving splinters into his heart. The force of the bullet drove him back as if he had been kicked by a mule. Reaction caused his throwing arm to come forward and release the knife but it fell harmlessly to the floor.

The acid smell of the burnt gun powder hung in the air. The silence was heavy, as was the fear in the hearts and faces of the living. Sister Teresa looked at the dead man and then at the smoking gun in her hand. What had she done? Had it been necessary? It had all happened so fast, she had not had time to think, only to react.

It was as if the world was standing still and she was spinning around. She could still see the surprised look on his face when fire leaped from the revolver. The sound of the discharge in the closed room and the sickening sound of the slug as it ripped through flesh and bone. Her legs began to buckle, sweat broke out on her forehead. She thought she would vomit and may have had she taken another look at the dead man.

Fact was, if she hadn't squeezed the trigger, it would have been her with the knife drove to the hilt in her chest. She would be dead and who knows how many more.

The story of the shooting at St. Anthony's spread like a wild prairie fire. Burning hotter on the fuel fed it by those who repeated the story. The story made this nun blindingly beautiful. Everyone loved the thought of a nun from the Catholic Mission stopping the bandits with a gun hand equal to that of a man.

It made all the papers and a dime novel was even written about this Maverick Nun.

Chapter Thirty

"That you're Sister?" Red asked.

The mining camp of Cripple Creek buzzed with continuous stories from up and down the trail. If a man could enter a saloon with a story no one else knew, he was the center of attention. The better the story, the more attention and free drinks he received. For that reason it wasn't at all unusual to spice up the story a trifle.

Bona gave Red a look of displeasure. He could disregard the question but he couldn't disregard his thoughts. A day didn't go by that he didn't think of her. He even thought of her at times when he was with Jayne. Now this story. The story didn't surprise him, he knew she could be as tough as the situation demanded. What he didn't like was the sarcasm and insolent jokes that accompanied the story.

"Just before she pulled the trigger she told him, 'Here's your ticket to Hell,' and then she shot him dead center."

Bona shock his head in disgust. There was no need to provoke trouble and say he didn't believe the story. That would only add more fuel to the fire. So Bona, was relieved when the subject was changed.

"You hear about the army surgeon at Fort Logan?" the cocky boldness of the man's voice told everyone he knew something they didn't.

"No, what'd he do?" The bartender wanted to get in on this new rumor. His job depended on him knowing the latest news.

"He murdered the commandant's wife." The man was dressed like a tin-horn gambler or a drummer for some company.

"The doc murdered the commanding officer's wife?" The barkeep wiped the bar waiting for more information.

"That's right. I was just there a few days ago. Army's got patrols out in every direction." He sipped his drink, enjoying the interest he had created. "She had been ill, suffering something trouble. This doc was giving her medicine that didn't help. The Commandant had decided to send her to Denver for treatment. Before he could, this doctor kills her."

"I don't know about you Bona but I'm about ready to go see what Tommy's up to. He should have that list of supplies you gave him loaded." Red downed his drink with a gulp and put the glass on the bar.

"Sure, I'm ready." Bona finished his drink and turned to leave. The man was still pushing his story.

"The army will get him and when they do I'd sure hate to be in his boots." Red stepped back to allow Bona to go first through the swinging batwing doors.

"He rides this big mule, so he won't be hard to spot." Red knew what the man was saying and yet he barely heard and understood so he felt sure Bona had not heard him talk about Maud. He was glad he had driven the wagon and that Maud was back in the valley.

The sun hit them like a giant ball of fire, so bright a man had to squint to see. It was enough to take a person's mind off what had been said inside.

At the General Store, they found Tommy sucking on rock candy and looking with longing eyes at a silver studded saddle. The goods were all loaded, the major part of the load was oats but there was also some staple items for the house.

Red did a little shopping while Bona and Tommy checked the load of supplies. He came out with a package under his arm and a sneaky smile on his face.

"I'll be right with you guys, got to stop in at the stage office a minute." He was gone before either Tommy or Bona could reply.

Just a mile or so out of town, they came upon a man sprawled out in the middle of the road. Red pulled up the team and Bona jumped off Buck to see what had happened.

"Looks like he was ambushed, two or three men. Shot him out of the saddle and took off with his horse and what money he had." Bona was reading the ground for sign while Red knelt beside the victim.

"How is he?" Tommy called from his horse.

"He's still alive but he has lost a lot of blood."

"Where's he hit?" Bona was still reading the ground.

"High in the chest, missed his lung and heart." Red had the man's shirt torn away and was applying pressure to the wound. The man was in a bad way, mighty near death. He attempted to speak but could manage only weak animal like sounds.

"Anything we can do?" Bona walked over to where Red was knelling over the man.

"Tommy, get one of those new towels and bring it here." The slug had passed clean through, leaving a gaping hole in the man's back. "Bring a bottle of the brandy too."

Red used the brandy to sterilize the wound and his pocket knife. He ripped the towel and used his knife to pack the wound. The hole in the back took two strips to pack it full. Using the remained of the towel Red formed a bandage. He forced a little brandy between the man's lips and took a long pull on the bottle himself before handing it to Bona.

"That's about all we can do for him besides getting him to town and a doctor."

They lifted him as gentle as they could and put him on top of the sacks of oats. Tommy tied his horse on behind and rode in the wagon to hold him as stead as possible. While Red turned the team back toward town, Bona kicked Buck into a lope and rode ahead to have help ready when they arrived. The man was so pale it scared Tommy. Red had to hold the team to a walk to make the ride smooth, the man could not stand too much jolting.

The man Cripple Creek called Doc Forest, was really nothing more than the undertaker who was experienced in treating gunshot wounds. If his treatment failed, he applied his second talent.

"You fixed him up real good. If he don't make it, it's sure not your fault." Forest was a short, dark and heavy set man who was always sweating. His office was above the funeral parlor so if death came, he could be fitted with a pine box downstairs.

"If the shock don't kill him, he should pull through." Red started for the door. Bona and Tommy were already down the long flight of stairs.

Standing at the wagon was a man with a star pinned to his vest. His shirttails hung out from under the leather vest. A number of others had arrived, miners and town's people curious to lean the details.

"Where did you find him?" The lawman asked.

"Just a mile or so outside of town." Bona swung up on Buck.

"See any sign of who did it or of this outfit?"

"No. Tracks showed two or three riders. They shot him out of his saddle and took everything with them."

Red climbed to the spring seat of the wagon and packed his pipe before taking up the reins.

"Will he live to tell what happened?" a tall, thin miner with long blond hair asked.

"Got a chance," Red replied as he put a match to his pipe.

"I'll go up so I can be there if and when he comes around." The lawman started for the stairs. The people were absorbed with the apparent robbery and attempted murder. This sort of thing happened all too frequently. They drifted away slowly talking among themselves.

The road was nothing more than wagon ruts with grass in the middle. The mountains were dark shadows, the top ridge so high Tommy had to lean back and raise his head to see it. A stream next to the road rolled over rocks, making pools where it paused, then rushing on again. A covey of quail burst into the air and sped away. One was too slow. A hawk hit it and feathers flew as the quail fell to the ground. A moment later the hawk rose with the dead quail clutched in his claws.

That hawk killed the poor quail," Tommy exclaimed.

"He got the slow one. That way the slow will not raise others who are slow. The hawk will also eat thousands of ground rats who eat the eggs of the quail. So he helps the quail more than he hurts them." Red puffed his pipe while giving Tommy a lesson in nature.

Soon they entered their valley. The cabin set back in the big trees with the mountain at its back and with the big welcoming porch running clear across the front was an impressive sight. After a quick meal Tommy went to his bunk. The deer hide webbing stretched on the frame of hickory posts provided a springy softness that soon had him asleep.

The pine knots in the fireplace sputtered and flickered shadows around the room. Bona paced but inevitability he had to ask the question.

"Why? Why did you kill that lady?" He shifted from one foot to the other, restraining his impatience best he could.

"That lady was my kid sister. She was dying, inch by inch. She was in pain, great pain. I heard her pray to die. To end her suffering. I watched her go from a strong healthy woman to nothing but skin and bones. She was in such pain she couldn't sleep." Red took a keep drag on his pipe and leaned against the cabin wall.

"Yes, I killed her. I killed her because I loved her. My brother-in-law planned to take her to Denver where she would linger and suffer even more. She would be with a stranger." Red stared, unseeing into the flickering fireplace.

"I'm sorry Red. I had no right to ask." Bona muttered the words tonelessly.

"I know it was murder but I look at it as an act of mercy. I'll drift." He reached for his coat on a peg by the door.

"Why?" Bona questioned.

"Why? Because you can't have a killer living here." His lips barely moved, his voice raspy.

"Who am I to judge?" Bona walked to Red and put his hand on his shoulder. "I knew there was a reason but I still had no right to ask."

"She was incurably ill, it was an act of love but it was still murder." When he said the word his lips quivered with a trembling motion. It took all his will power to keep from crying.

"A man must live the best way he knows how. Do the things that seem to be right for the time and place. I have done many things I am not proud of." Bona went to the fire and poured each a cup of coffee. He laced it with a shot of brandy and handed one cup to Red. The steaming coffee and brandy tasted good. Neither spoke. They had an understanding beyond words. They were friends. This was a wild and untamed country, you had to sidestep the law once in a while to apply true justice.

"Red, I want you to know you are welcome here as long as you wish to stay."

"Thanks. She was the only family I have."

"Well, I guess the three of us have that in common."

The next morning they made a swing of the valley checking the stock. They stopped by a small stream for lunch. There were patches of wild berries all around, so Tommy took his hat to pick some.

"How do it tell which ones are poison?" He stood at the edge of a patch, waiting for one of them to answer.

"Just watch the birds. Any you see them not eating, you best not eat." Red walked over to where Tommy was. Seeing some wild onions, he took his knife and dug them from the ground. He would take them back near the cabin and replant them.

"You can see where the birds have been feeding. A bird won't feed on poison berries." Red pointed to places where the birds had cleaned off the ripe berries.

"How do the birds know the good berries?"

"That's a good question Tommy and I don't know the answer to it."

"I wish Sister Teresa was here. Then we would have a real family." Red glanced at Bona to see if there was any reaction.

"The boy could be right. It might be the right time for you to ride down to the mission and let her know how we are doing."

"Yeah, how about just going to see her?" Tommy had his mouth half full of berries.

"Hell's fire. You guys are about to use up my patience." He took out a cheroot and a twig from the fire provided the flame. "She is doing what is important to her and what she wants to do. Anyway, I am kind of interested in Jayne." He took a deep drag on his smoke and missed the look Tommy gave Red.

"What? You can't compare...." Tommy never got to finish, the look he got from Bona put fear in his heart and silenced his tongue.

"I have had enough of you guy's philosophy and advice." Tommy and Red knew better than to attempt to pursue the issue.

They could also see why Bona was impressed with Jayne. She vigorously represented the strong, sleek woman of the West. She seemed to be always "on-stage" when around Bona. She had a way of making him feel important, like the star of her life.

Jayne had all the right moves and said all the correct things. She had a great deal to offer any man. Riding her wave of energy they could carve out a destiny.

A thousand years ago, man set forth at the first light of dawn to conquer a meal. Soon, even our club-wielding ancestors learned man did not live by meat alone. The true joys of life came when he shared his world with a woman. Red was too old, Tommy too young. Bona was like a lobo searching for a mate.

Life had been so simple when sex was just a physical, sweaty workout. Sister Teresa and Jayne mysteriously changed that. Life was intensified and intimate. It had a new and deeper dimension. Bona was confused, did he like Jayne because he couldn't have Sister Teresa?

He looked out over the valley. He had handled the hardships. The Indians, the weather, the lawlessness, these were easy compared to this problem. He didn't know the answer but he knew for sure he did not want any more advice, direction or guidance from Red and Tommy.

A woman could be like finding a vein of pure gold. Gold has a power of its own over men. So does the thoughts of a good woman. A good woman was like the fireworks on the fourth of July.

He did not sleep well that night, seemed to be anxious to get up and start a new day. The next morning Bona walked out on the big porch. He had plenty. More than at any time in his life. He had horses, cattle, land and two good friends. He had a place most anyone would be proud of. He was still as empty as when he drifted like a tumbleweed. He had a churning inside that said this wasn't enough. He had always been a risk taker, it could be time to take another.

"Red. Can you and Tommy hold down the fort for a spell?" He called to Red who was just coming out the door.

"Sure."

"I got something to do, it will only take a few days."

"You go do what you got to do, we will handle things."

Bona quickly packed a few things, saddled Buck and rode down the valley. He felt better already. He felt like he did when drifting through Texas. He was in search of something again. He pulled his hat brim lower to shade his eyes from the morning sun.

Pausing at the gate, to take another look back at the cabin. He thought he could see Tommy waving but at that distance it was difficult to tell.

Chapter Thirty-one

What a difference a split second, a squeeze of a trigger could make. It ended one life and sent another to prison, but most of all, it made a celebrity out of Sister Teresa. As the story spread, travelers rode out of their way to stop at the mission. Even non-believers wanted to kneel before the now famous crucifix.

The children didn't have to worry about selling pottery and candles in the East. People were flocking to the mission and buying faster than they could produce. They all wanted to meet the now famous nun. This Maverick Nun who could shoot the eyes out of a rattlesnake at fifty yards. They all wanted a piece of art to sell to a less fortunate friends who couldn't make it to the mission.

Sister Teresa was not pleased by this new attention caused by a twist of fate. She spent as much of her time as was physically possible alone and away from the curious, meddling people. It made it almost impossible for her to be the teacher she had been. She knew it had been either kill or be killed. She had made her peace with that. It was the spreading of this tale and the celebrity status she couldn't handle.

At first she was angry but she learned that anger was a sign that something was wrong. The chain of events had placed her in a position where she was no longer Sister Teresa. The turmoil, the spreading tale was something so non-traditional she could not function.

Several days earlier, she had received a package. Inside was the most beautiful wedding dress she had ever seen. White satin with lace. It was what every bride would love to wear. She had been reluctant to touch it. Behind locked doors she got up the courage to put it on. It fit like it was made for her. She felt so good, like the first time she put on her habit.

There was a day, not long ago when she was needed here at the mission. Now, she felt the best thing she could do for the mission was to leave. She talked with Father Joseph and she prayed.

She was at the altar praying when a boy came and announced that a man was at the gate to see her. He was riding a big buckskin horse and looked as if he could be dangerous.

She felt a warm, nurturing excitement surge through her. It was time, it was time for a change. Her prayers had been answered.

The door opened and she appeared on the steps. She was lovely. A lump formed in Bona's throat. Never had he felt the way he did at this moment. He remembered the first time they met. The times she was a pain in the butt and the many times she was a special comfort. He was sure he had special feelings for this woman and now he felt sure she returned his feelings.

She was dressed in white, a white wedding dress. He didn't know where she got it or how she knew but he had never been happier. He jumped off Buck and ran to her. She was in his arms to the cheers of the children.

Epilogue

Tommy got his wish to be a part of a regular family when Sister Teresa became Fran King.

Red lived out his days in the valley and his medical talent came in handle several times.

Other works by Ken Wilbur

Blue Eagle: The story of a young Confederate soldier at the end of the Civil War and his black stallion, Blue Eagle.

Eagle Brand: The story of three Colorado men going to Texas and finding more than they bargained for.

Eagle Valley: Is the story of how Native Americans and White settlers could live together in peace to the point of helping each other to survive.

Eagle Flight: The story of a young baseball player from the little town of Randalia, Iowa going to Chicago to play baseball for the Chicago White Stocking, entwined with the story of a young nun leaving the order to find out who murdered her father.

Luta: The story of a young man who is half Cheyenne and how he learns to deal with it.

These books may be purchased on line at Authorhouse.com or by calling 888-519-5121

Printed in the United States
By Bookmasters